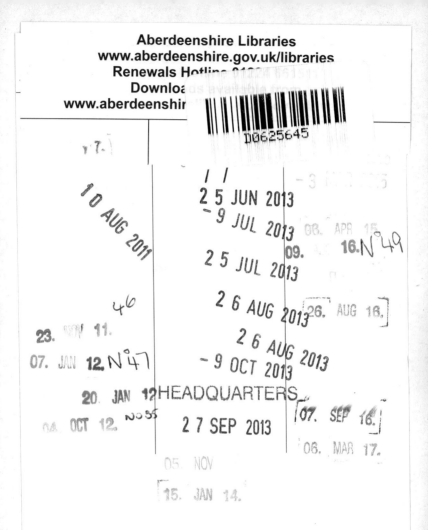

# FOR THE CHILDREN'S SAKE

Cathy Galliani wakes in hospital, after a car accident, to learn that her husband Vittorio is dead and her stepchildren are with his family in Italy. She is visited in hospital by Dan Kirby, a witness to the accident. Cathy travels to Italy to see the children, but when Dan follows her he ends up in hospital himself. And as his life hangs in the balance, Cathy realises how deeply he cares for her — and who he really is . . .

TERESA ASHBY

# FOR THE CHILDREN'S SAKE

*Complete and Unabridged*

**LINFORD**
*Leicester*

First published in Great Britain

First Linford Edition
published 2011

British Library CIP Data

Ashby, Teresa.
  For the children's sake. - -
  (Linford romance library)
  1. Stepfamilies- -Fiction. 2. Traffic accident
  victims- -Fiction. 3. Witnesses- -Fiction.
  4. Italy- -Fiction. 5. Love stories.
  6. Large type books.
  I. Title II. Series
  823.9'2–dc22

  ISBN 978–1–44480–641–0          **LP**

Published by
F. A. Thorpe (Publishing)
Anstey, Leicestershire

Set by Words & Graphics Ltd.
Anstey, Leicestershire
Printed and bound in Great Britain by
T. J. International Ltd., Padstow, Cornwall

This book is printed on acid-free paper

# 1

For some time Cathy had been aware that she was in a hospital, although her mind was still too weak to question why.

Everything was so wrong, so alien, that she was forced to slam a door in her mind and bury the unacceptable truth.

Now a voice was penetrating the darkness — a persistent, demanding voice — which dragged her, against her will, away from blissful unreality into the waking nightmare she knew awaited her.

Try as she might, she could no longer go on ignoring the voice.

'Cathy . . . Cathy Galliani . . . '

Slowly she forced her eyes open and found her vision, at first, distorted and blurred. Sound was strange, too, as if she were floating under water.

She didn't want to think, didn't want to remember, she didn't want to *know* about the events which had brought her here.

'Hello, Sleeping Beauty. So, you're awake at last, are you?'

Gradually, she became painfully aware of the rest of her body.

Her ribs ached and her hand throbbed and, when she looked down at it, she saw a bandage holding an intravenous drip tube tightly in place.

'Just glucose and vitamins, love,' the nurse explained brightly.

'I know,' she managed to whisper through parched lips. 'I used to be a nurse.'

'Good. Then you'll know there's absolutely nothing to be frightened of! Are you comfortable enough?'

'My legs feel strange,' she said slowly, 'and everything hurts.'

'Well, you did knock yourself about a bit.' The nurse smiled. 'But you'll mend. From all accounts, you were lucky to get away as lightly as you did . . . ' She broke off abruptly.

Awareness was flooding back now with almost indecent speed, and rising panic began to well inside as Cathy desperately fought to keep the truth from the forefront of her mind.

No matter how hard she tried, it was impossible to fight it back and with the vivid realisation of what had happened, came sudden, brutal, wide-awake consciousness.

'My husband!' she cried, grabbing the nurse's arm tightly, despite her weakness. 'Nurse, my children . . . Stefano . . . Paolina!'

She tried to get out of the bed, but she was much too weak and only succeeded in sending the intravenous unit crashing to the floor.

The nurse, with amazing speed and dexterity, managed in turn, to summon help, right the i.v. unit and hold Cathy in the bed.

Suddenly the door flew open and another nurse rushed in, followed by a young doctor, his white coat flapping open as he hurried towards the bed, his eyes, quickly assessing the damage.

'Doctor . . . ' Cathy gasped, pleading with her wide, terror-filled eyes for an answer to the questions she knew she must ask.

'I want to know what has happened to my husband and children,' she said, trying to disguise her mounting panic. 'What am I doing here?'

And she began to struggle once more.

'We may as well remove this drip altogether now, Nurse,' the doctor said to the first nurse, the one with the loud, jolly voice.

Then, turning back to Cathy, he said, 'Now, Mrs Galliani, perhaps you could take a few deep breaths and settle yourself.'

This is it, Cathy thought, panic welling again. This is where I get the bad news and I don't want it . . . I don't . . .

'My name is Dr Campbell,' the young man began, adopting a more friendly tone as he sat down on the bed beside her. 'I've been looking after you, Mrs Galliani.'

He lifted her limp hand and examined the bruise left by the drip. 'Tsk! You didn't help that, you know.'

'I just want to know what has happened to my family,' she said through gritted teeth.

She was struggling again, this time to hold back her tears as she waited for the young doctor to say the words that would shape her future.

'Do you remember anything at all, Mrs Galliani? How much can you tell me?'

'We were on our way to Vittorio's parents' house, outside Naples.' She broke off to smile weakly.

'Vittorio said he wanted me to see as much of his homeland as I could before we got to his parents, but I thought he was stalling for time. He seemed reluctant to . . .'

Her smile disappeared as quickly as it had come.

'We were driving on a motorway. He

said it would be quicker than a minor road and . . . safer.' She broke off.

Safer! How ironic! How very wrong!

Vittorio *had* been taking his time getting to his parents' home, but once they were on the road, he seemed in a mad rush to get the visit over with as quickly as possible.

'The children were asleep in the back of the hired car. Vittorio was driving and I was worried because he seemed so tense.

'The kids had hardly slept at all on the plane.' Her smile returned as she momentarily blocked out the bad memory. 'They were so excited about seeing their father's family . . . '

Cathy's smile faded again as she went on. 'Anyway, we were driving along, had just looked over my shoulder at the children and when I turned . . . suddenly . . . '

She threw up her hands in front of her face as recollection and reality became one and the same in her tired, confused mind.

'Headlights! Coming straight for us. Oh, God! Vittorio . . . He swerved, but it was too late . . . I screamed — but it was too late.

'Everything slowed down then, as if we were living in a bad dream. It was as though it was happening in slow motion. Do you know what I mean, Doctor?'

He nodded, but said nothing, allowing Cathy to go on.

'The other car ploughed into us on Vittorio's side, then our car was turning over and over and over . . . Then there was nothing.

'It lasted for ages. Then came a horrible, endless silence, broken only by the sounds of a wheel spinning and something dripping . . . petrol, I think. Yes, I could smell petrol. Then I heard Paolina crying.'

She took another deep breath and closed her eyes.

'I called Vittorio, but he was so still beside me. His head was slumped forward. There was blood trickling down his face, but I couldn't get to him because my legs were trapped and there was a great weight on my chest . . .

'Little Paolina was so frightened. I talked to her, but I couldn't move.

'Then I heard another vehicle and things began to go dark . . . I could taste blood in my mouth and I heard someone shouting . . . 'Presto . . . presto . . . ambulanza . . .''

'I don't . . . I can't remember any more. I'm sorry.'

She began to sob bitterly, her body slumped as at last she gave way to weakness.

Vittorio must be dead and for all she knew, so was little Stefano. And what had become of Paolina? Had she been terribly hurt?

'They had to cut you from the wreckage.' The doctor spoke gently, taking up the story where Cathy's own memory failed her.

'Obviously, you've damaged your legs a bit. But don't worry — given care and time, everything will be fine.

'Although there was extensive bruising to your back, I'm happy to tell you that your spinal cord wasn't injured in any way. You suffered three broken ribs, a little internal damage and numerous other minor injuries.

'As far as we can tell at this stage, there's no reason to believe you won't make a full and good recovery.

'But you must understand, Mrs Galliani, we have to keep you here until we're sure . . . '

'Here?' Suddenly, Cathy stopped sobbing and she turned to stare at the doctor. 'What's going on?'

A worse fear began to claw at her. 'Why am I here? I was in Italy . . . '

'Calm yourself.' The doctor turned his pale-brown eyes away.

'Your husband had taken out insurance so that, in the event of illness or accident, you or your family would be brought back to England.

'You spent a week in Italy before it was felt safe to bring you over here and you've been with us for three weeks now.'

'What happened to my husband, Dr Campbell?'

'I'm sorry,' he said softly, once again avoiding her eyes. 'I was told he died instantly. He would have known nothing.'

The pain, although she had been expecting it, was like a physical blow to the pit of her stomach.

How could he be dead? Why? How could their blissfully happy life together be cut so short?

'And my children?' she whispered.

'Your children?' He looked puzzled.

'Yes, Doctor, my children — Paolina and Stefano. They were in the car with us.'

'Oh, the Galliani children. They're fine, just fine.' He smiled for the first time.

'Mrs Galliani, you were a nurse. A staff nurse? Then I shouldn't have to tell you about taking things easy at first, should I?

'The little girl had some stitches in her arm and the boy had a very minor head injury but, all things considered, they came out of the accident virtually unscathed.

'Being asleep and therefore totally relaxed probably helped.'

'They're so young to have lost their father . . . Oh, Doctor, let me see them.'

'Look at yourself.' He was back on familiar ground and speaking with his previous calmness. 'You're in no fit state to take care of yourself, let alone two young children.'

'But if they're here, in the hospital, couldn't I just . . . ?'

'They are with their grandparents in Italy. It seemed best.'

'Yes . . . yes,' she agreed, relieved. 'There's no-one else. I have no family and all Vittorio's people are over there.'

Happy in the knowledge that the children would be well taken care of until she was well enough to do so herself, Cathy relaxed once again.

'I'm going to ask the nurse to give you a sedative now,' the doctor said patiently. 'Once you've had more rest, you'll begin to feel better. The worst is over now, Mrs Galliani.'

'I'll go back to Italy,' she said sleepily, 'as soon as I'm fit. And I'll collect the children.'

'Of course you will.'

She was barely aware of the nurse bending over her and giving her an injection, hardly aware of her own voice murmuring as sleep took over.

'Stefano . . . Paolina . . . ' . . . And with the memories, the dream began.

★ ★ ★

They looked like angels lying there and Cathy said so. The girl's long, black curls fanned out around her head, shining softly in the light from the landing to form a shimmering halo.

The boy lay in infant abandon, his arms wide open, his face upturned and flushed a healthy pink. His hair was almost white, in striking contrast to his tanned skin.

'They always look like angels when

they're sleeping.' Vittorio smiled down at her, a world of tenderness in his eyes as he put his arm around her. 'But when they're awake, they're like little devils!'

'I can't believe that,' she whispered, taking a final look at the two peaceful children before allowing Vittorio to draw her gently from the room.

'So now you know my terrible secret.' He put his arm around her and pulled her close to him, so close that she could feel the steady, strong beat of his heart.

'Do you still love me? Do you still want to be my wife?'

'I do and I do!' She laughed. 'But I feel hurt that you didn't tell me about your children before. Didn't you trust me, Vittorio?'

'You are still young, Catriana.' He moved away to the window and turned his back on her.

'You are only twenty-three, too young to be the mother of a seven-year-old girl; and a boy, not yet three and missing his mother so badly . . .

'You may not like them! Heaven forbid, they may not like you! The years ahead could be full of untold difficulties.'

'What happened to their mother?'

She knew that her question would be painful for him, but she had to ask it anyway.

If she was to marry him, be the mother of his children, then she had to know everything about him. There should be no secrets.

'My wife, Viviana, died two years ago. Stefano was only a few months old, but aware enough to be deeply affected when the most important person in his life was suddenly taken away. Her decline had been rapid since his birth.

'When she was pregnant, they found, in some routine blood tests, that she had a rare blood disease. She refused treatment while she was pregnant, and afterwards . . . it was too late.'

'I'm so sorry, Vittorio.' She hurried towards him, standing at his side by the window and resting her head against him.

He turned to take her in his arms and almost as soon as his face was close to hers, his lips about to touch her own, his image began to fade . . .

★ ★ ★

Cathy reached out wildly in the darkness, trying to cling to him, but already his face was gone, and in its place there was only the soft light of the night lamp above her bed.

'Vittorio . . . ' Her voice was no more than a hoarse, strangled whisper in the night, unheard by all but herself.

The curtains were closed, the room full of misty shadows and, in the distance, she could hear the night sounds.

She wasn't even aware that she was crying until she felt the hot tears trickling down her face. She thought of Paolina and Stefano and her heart gave a painful twist. How were they coping?

Stefano had become so dependent on her over the past year or so and she prayed that his grandparents would understand if his problems returned, as they probably would.

If he ever retreated back into that tense world in which he lived when she first knew him, where he stammered nervously, goodness knew how long it would take to coax him back out again.

'Hello, I had a feeling that you were awake.' Cathy looked up, startled, and saw that a young nurse had popped her head around the door, her smile warm, friendly.

'I'd really love a cup of tea, Nurse.' Cathy smiled.

'Then you shall have one. Just hold on, I've got a pot brewing right now. By the way, my name's Susan. No need for us to be formal, is there?' She smiled kindly to Cathy as she went out.

She returned quickly, the brisk swish of her uniform the only sound now in that lonely night.

'Here you are. Do you need help sitting up? Ribs still painful, are they?' She adjusted the back rest and helped

Cathy to a half-sitting position. 'You used to be a nurse, I believe?'

'That's right — and my name's Cathy, by the way. I met Vittorio when I was nursing.'

'Your husband?'

'He was brought in as an emergency appendix, would you believe?' She smiled, the smile turning to a laugh as she remembered how she and Vittorio first met. 'He was the most awkward . . .

'He was the manager of a large hotel and was absolutely desperate to get back to work. He was convincd the whole place would fall apart.

'We practically had to tie him to his bed and you know what Italians are like! He used to throw his arms about as he talked and knock everything flying off his locker!'

She laughed out loud. 'Oh, he was so funny and yet, sometimes, he was so serious and solemn.'

'Go on,' the nurse prompted when Cathy fell silent.

'He came here from his home just outside Naples when he was twenty-one. He was already married to Viviana, his first wife, and he took a job as a waiter in the restaurant at The Brenton Hotel.

'Vittorio wasn't the kind of man to stay a waiter for long and, within four years, he was under manager. By the time I met him, he was manager and the owner, Malcolm Edgar, was obviously earmarking him for bigger and better things.'

'Wow!' The nurse grinned. 'It all sounds pretty high powered. Anyway, go on, about Vittorio. Was he divorced when you met him?'

'No,' Cathy said quickly. 'Absolutely not! He was a widower.'

'So, you must have been to Italy lots of times. I do envy you, Cathy.'

'Well, you needn't,' Cathy said thoughtfully. 'There's nothing to envy. It was my first-ever visit when . . . when we had the accident.'

Her face crumpled beneath the

sudden weight of over-whelming grief as it all came flooding back.

'Have you finished your tea?' The nurse stood and took the half-empty cup from Cathy's shaking hands.

'Nurse, I mean, Susan . . . I . . . ' Cathy began shakily.

'I know, Cathy. I know.' She squeezed Cathy's bruised hand ever so gently, but even that small pressure was enough to make Cathy wince with pain. 'You look very tired and I think it's time you went back to sleep. I'm off duty now, but I'll be back in the morning. Buzz for the night nurse if you need anything.'

'Thank you,' Cathy murmured and slipped quickly once more into her fitful sleep.

That girl needs help, Susan mused as she hurried down the long hospital corridor. Not just for her physical problems — she needs someone who'll bring her out of herself . . . I wish I could do more.

★ ★ ★

19

This time, when the dream came, Cathy found herself at Heathrow Airport.

Vittorio was more uptight than she'd ever known him.

Normally, he was easy going, taking an almost laid-back view of life, except for his work.

'Why don't you just admit it, Vittorio? You don't want to go, do you?' she said candidly.

'Come on, it sticks out a mile! You've done nothing but delay this trip and now you're taking the longest possible route.'

'If I had wanted to do that, Catarina, I would have taken the ferry to Holland and driven all the way.'

'I honestly think you would have done that, too, but you said the traffic was chaotic at this time of year.'

'Ah, Catarina, let us not argue about this,' he pleaded. 'We are going to enjoy ourselves and I shall show you all the sights of my country.'

'And see your family,' she added.

'My family . . . ' His face darkened.

'Yes, we shall meet with the family.'

She still hadn't yet figured out why Vittorio was so reluctant to take her to meet his family.

She thought they wouldn't approve of her and when she'd said that, he had told her quite firmly, 'They will love you, as I do.'

And his sentiments were confirmed when she'd received a telephone call out of the blue from a close member of his family.

'Hello, Catarina.' The Italian-accented voice on the phone had been unfamiliar. 'Is Vittorio there?'

'No. I'm afraid he's not.'

'A pity. I shall telephone later, yes? Tell him that Uncle Marco called, would you?'

'I'll do that,' she'd said, relief flooding through her. His voice had been friendly, and held no hint of the animosity she had feared from the Galliani family.

'And, Catarina, tell my nephew that I shall wish to meet his new wife.' He'd laughed. 'We have heard much about you through his letters and are eager to meet you.'

But, when she'd told Vittorio about the call, instead of being happy as she had expected, his reaction had been almost panic stricken.

'What did he say? Catarina, what did he want?'

'He's going to call back. Why, what's wrong?'

'Everything!' He'd slumped into a chair and rested his face in his hands. 'Why can't they leave me alone? I have my own life to lead.'

'What do you mean?'

'It's nothing. I told you before . . . they wanted me to go into the family business — that is all. Wine! Pff! Is not for me. I came to England to . . .'

'Escape?'

He'd looked up at her sharply then, the animosity in his eyes most unexpected, and was about to answer her, when the telephone bell shrilled.

Vittorio had jumped, his face paling as he'd reached for the receiver and picked it up.

'Pronto!' He'd spoken in Italian and continued to do so. Cathy only understood the occasional word.

His usually-dark face was ashen, his mood subdued, and Cathy left him alone so she could get supper for the children.

'Catarina.' Vittorio had come into the kitchen, his shirt open at the neck, his tie loosened. 'We have to go out this evening. Would you arrange for some-one to look after the children?'

'Of course, but where are we going?'

'My Uncle Marco is in London. He wishes us to meet him at his hotel for dinner.'

Uncle Marco was tall, taller even than Vittorio and he'd stood with his back to them as thcy'd entered his hotel suite, looking out of the window.

When he'd turned, Cathy had gasped, for his resemblance to Vittorio was quite startling — only the silver flecks in his hair had betrayed the difference in their ages.

'Vittorio . . . Catarina . . . ' He'd rushed forward to greet them, taking first his nephew, then Cathy in a massive embrace.

'Come, sit . . . sit. I have ordered dinner to be served here. But first we talk.'

Occasionally, Marco had spoken in Italian and Vittorio's face had reddened and Cathy had gone cold as his eyes dropped to stare at the floor.

Vittorio was a powerful man, yet apparently he was terrified of his own uncle!

'I have told him that his father misses him.' Uncle Marco had turned to explain to Cathy.

'I am asking him to come home, for a visit,' Marco had gone on. 'You will do that, Vittorio? Bring Catarina and the children.'

'Yes, Uncle Marco,' Vittorio had said, and Cathy had stared at him in open amazement.

Throughout her months of pleading he had constantly said no, yet this man, this uncle from Italy, had persuaded him to return in a few short minutes!

\* \* \*

'You ate some breakfast this morning.'

Cathy looked up, shaken from her daydream by Dr Campbell.

'I must say, you're looking better already.' He glanced at her chart and nodded to Susan, the young nurse who had been so kind before.

Cathy smiled weakly up at Susan. The young nurse, while not stopping what she was doing, beamed encouragingly at Cathy.

But she waited until Dr Campbell had left before saying suddenly. 'You know, Cathy, you may not think it but things could have been much worse.'

'Dr Campbell told me yesterday that you probably owe your life to the quick thinking of a young Englishman who was behind you on the motorway and saw the whole accident.'

Cathy looked up suddenly, startled by this new information.

At first, Cathy didn't know what to say. For, try as she might, she could not remember anyone helping her at the scene of the crash.

But now she sent up a silent prayer of thanks to that unknown Englishman who'd apparently done so much.

Then, as she was leaving, Susan turned back and said, 'By the way, there's a letter for you. I left it on the locker.'

Cathy looked up and saw the envelope, her mood quickly lightening when she saw the Italian stamp.

It was bound to be from the Gallianis, no doubt with news of the children, perhaps even telling her when it would be convenient to collect them.

Her heart was thundering as she ripped the envelope in order to read the letter within.

With trembling fingers, she opened the neatly-folded sheet and let the ragged envelope fall to the floor.

She hadn't realised just how much she was smiling until the grin froze on her face, a ridiculous gesture given the cold formality of the letter.

It was short and to the point, from the Gallianis' lawyer, and she had to read and re-read the words several times before their meaning sunk in.

★   ★   ★

*Dear Signora Galliani,*

*I am writing to you on behalf of my clients, Signor Silvano and Signora Marianna Galliani.*

*My clients are happy that your recovery is good and wish to inform you that the funeral of their son has already taken place at home.*

*I would inform you that the children of Vittorio will be staying in Italy with their family as you, not being their natural mother, have no claim to them, legal or otherwise.*

*It would be wise of you to start your*

*life anew and forget your connections with the Galliani family.*

*Wishing you a continued recovery.*

*Sincerely,*
*Guido Rossi.*

It was too much for Cathy! She screwed up the paper in her hand while tears silently fell from her eyes.

Vittorio was dead and buried, the children were miles away in a strange country — strange even to them — and there was *nothing* she could do!

She was suddenly shaking all over, her whole body trembling with anger and fear.

'Stefano! . . . ' she screamed . . . 'Paolina! . . . ' her voice the cry of an injured animal which echoed along the hospital corridors, chilling the blood of all who heard.

'Vittorio . . . ' she called out forlornly.

By the time the door flew open, she was in deep despair, tears streaming down her face.

Susan and another nurse held her while the doctor administered a sedative.

'What's upset her like this?' the senior of the nurses asked.

'It must be that letter,' Susan declared, glancing anxiously at her patient.

Cathy could hear Susan saying over and over again, 'It's all right, Cathy. It's all right . . . '

She tried to answer, tried to beg for their help, tell them why she was upset but the drug was working fast, seeping through her body like advancing sleep.

The medical staff stayed with Cathy until she became totally relaxed.

'She'll be fine now. Leave her.' The doctor's voice grew distant as her eyelids closed.

Reluctantly, Susan did as the doctor bid her. But, as she quietly closed the door to Cathy's room, she made a promise to herself and Cathy. Cathy desperately needed a friend — and Susan knew the very person who fitted the bill!

When next she awoke, slowly this time after a false, dreamless sleep, the afternoon sun was streaming in through the window and it was a while before Cathy became aware of the stranger at her bedside.

She stared at him curiously, her vision still blurred and unreliable from sleep.

He was no doctor, though, his clothes were far too casual — he wore a leather jacket.

Her vision cleared slightly and she saw he was her own age or perhaps just a little older and had a deep tan.

'Who are you?' she asked fearfully.

'My name is Dan Kirby,' he told her, smiling and half standing. 'How are you feeling, Mrs Galliani?'

She watched him suspiciously. 'What do you want?' she demanded.

'I'm sorry, I didn't mean to alarm you.' He sat down again on the edge of his chair. 'I was first on the scene after your accident. I was driving behind you.

'Once I'd told the Guardia all I knew and had seen that you were being taken care of in hospital, I went on my way, but I couldn't help wondering about you, especially with you being English and in a strange country.'

Cathy exhaled slowly, understanding gradually dawning on her. So this was her Good Samaritan! The man to whom she owed so much!

'Anyway, when I'd finished my business — I'm an art historian — I went to the hospital in Naples and they told me you'd been transported back here.'

Cathy had been watching Dan Kirby intently as he spoke. Now, at last, though, she found her voice and declared, rather emotionally, 'I can't thank you enough, Mr Kirby, for what you did.

'If you hadn't arrived on the scene when you did and helped the way you did, who knows, I might not have been alive today.

'But, you didn't have to come to see

me today. You've done enough already.'

'I was anxious to know how you were and, as soon as I'd finished working in Italy, I came home — I'd some holiday time due me.

'Also, I thought you'd like this back. I found it at the scene of the accident and put it in my pocket to give you when we reached the hospital. But, in all the confusion, it slipped my mind.'

He smiled at Cathy as he withdrew a gold locket and chain from his pocket and held it up in front of her.

Cathy gasped, instantly recognising the trinket. Then, almost too eagerly, she snatched the locket from his hand and, with trembling hands, opened it.

Inside, were two tiny photographs of Stefano and Paolina, taken only a few weeks ago. Cathy stared and stared at the miniature likenesses, her heart aching with love for the two mischievous faces smiling back at her.

'Oh, thank you, Mr Kirby. You don't know how much this means to me,' she whispered. 'Just to see their little faces brings them nearer to me, somehow.' She lapsed into silence, still staring at the locket, obviously lost in her own thoughts.

'You're very tired, Mrs Galliani, I'll go now.' The man stood up then.

'I'm sorry — I don't mean to be rude.' She forced a watery smile. 'Thank you for your concern. And for bringing this back to me.'

'It's OK. You've been through a lot and I'm really sorry about your husband. Look, I've written my telephone number on here.' He put a small piece of paper down on the locker. 'You can usually contact me there.'

She looked questioningly up at him.

He shrugged and smiled. 'Sometimes, it's nice to know that there's help at the end of a telephone line.'

He said goodbye and turned to go. Cathy turned away, glad he was going so that she could be alone with her thoughts.

She opened her other hand and found the letter still grasped there. She read it through again, half hoping she'd imagined the cruel words, that they were all part of some hideous night-mare.

There were no hysterics, no anguished screams now, just the plain sounds of heartbroken sobs as she re-read the letter.

Suddenly, she felt the touch of a hand on hers and looked up, startled, her eyes red and swollen, in her chalk-white face.

Dan Kirby was standing beside her bed, his face a mask of genuine concern.

His eyes glanced briefly at the crumpled letter in her hand. 'I don't know what it says,' he said gently. 'But I do know that you need help.'

★ ★ ★

Dan hurried down the hospital steps and walked briskly across the ground to where he had parked his car.

He hadn't meant to spend quite so long with the woman whose dark, sad eyes haunted him, still.

But, when he'd turned round and seen her, looking so miserable and hopeless, his heart had gone out to her. He'd coaxed her to speak.

And slowly, painfully, her whole story had come out. He had been genuinely touched when he realised what she must be going through. To lose her husband was bad enough, but never to see her children again . . .

Poor woman! Her whole world was collapsing around her. Reaching his car, he jumped in, still deep in thought and drove off quickly, aware that he still had a lot of work to do. Soon his car became part of the busy London traffic.

At last he turned into a quieter street and pulled up outside a modern office block.

Once inside, he hurried through a large, brightly-lit office, glancing round as he passed by, nodding at the few people who bothered to acknowledge his presence.

Pausing only to knock once on a half-glazed door before entering, he strode purposefully in.

'Close the door, Kirby!' The slim, middle-aged man behind the desk didn't even glance up from the sheaf of papers before him. 'Well, Kirby,' he said finally, raising his head to look at Dan with steel-grey eyes, 'did you make contact with the Galliani woman?'

'Yes, sir,' Dan replied quietly, a sudden, disturbing vision of two grief-stricken eyes springing to mind.

'Does she suspect anything?'

'No,' Dan said more firmly now. 'Not a thing.'

# 2

Cathy looked around the room, sure every little detail would be etched for ever on her mind by the time she left hospital.

Suddenly the door opened and a cleaner backed in, towing a large vacuum cleaner behind her.

She smiled briefly before setting to work and Cathy closed her eyes, listening to the drone of the vacuum as the woman worked.

Cathy's tired mind gradually drifted away, lulled by the monotonous sound which was so much like a car engine . . .

Vittorio was beside her and she had been staring at him for some time, not sure how to voice her concern. *Why* was he so tense?

'What's wrong?' she asked at last. '*Something's* troubling you. Why can't you tell me what it is? Have *I* done something wrong?'

'No, darling, you haven't done anything wrong. But you're right, there is something on my mind, something you have to know . . . '

'Then tell me,' she urged him, eager to share his worries and fears whatever they might be and perhaps help, too, if she could.

'It concerns my family. You'll have to tread carefully with them. They . . . they're . . . look, we'll stop soon and I promise we'll talk this through before we go on to the villa.'

Cathy remembered feeling reassured and worried all at once, but they had never had the opportunity to talk it through.

For, not long afterwards, the blinding headlights of another car appeared through the driving rain and Vittorio had been engaged in a desperate struggle to keep the car on the road.

The car had spun round and round on the slippery surface and, all the time, the threatening lights had come closer and closer.

Cathy had screamed and Vittorio failed to pull the car out of the skid and the black monster careered into them, turning their car over and over . . .

Then had come the darkness — the endless, lonely darkness, the smell of dripping petrol and the sound of a wheel spinning aimlessly, clicking monotonously as it turned, going nowhere.

It was almost hypnotic that sound, getting slowly louder, drowning out the others . . . Click, click! Click, click!

The sound was different now — faster, sharper somehow, and it seemed to be going round and round in her head, getting louder and louder . . .

She opened her eyes suddenly, not knowing where she was at first, unable to fathom the still-audible clicking sound.

She moved her head stiffly, slowly, as her memory gradually returned. Of course, her hospital room! But where was that noise coming from?

The cleaner had gone but, in the chair, in the corner, busily knitting, her fingers working so fast with needles and wool that they were almost a blur, sat a small, attractive, white-haired woman.

She started when she saw movement from the bed and quickly, but carefully, folded her knitting and pushed it into a large tapestry bag.

'You were asleep when I came in, dear,' she explained, 'and I didn't want to disturb you.

'I'm sorry I was late this morning.'

'Late?' Cathy said, puzzled, the last remnants of the nightmare finally fading.

The woman looked properly at Cathy then, and her hand covered her face as her mouth formed a round 'O' of surprise.

Her pale brown eyes widened and a faint flush spread through her powdered cheeks.

'Oh, my goodness,' she said at last. 'I've been sitting here all this time waiting for you to wake up . . . and you're not Mrs Matthews, are you?'

'No.' Cathy smiled, momentarily forgetting the pain of her vivid nightmare.

'Well, of course you're not! Mrs Matthews is eighty if she's a day. Have they moved her? This *is* room five, isn't it?'

'Six,' Cathy said patiently.

'Oh! Honestly. I think I need my head examined, sometimes! Never mind, now I'm here . . . '

'I don't understand,' Cathy said, feeling more confused than ever.

'I'm a hospital visitor; have been for some time now. I was supposed to be seeing old Mrs Matthews today, but . . . '

Cathy's amused smile froze on her lips. 'Sister asked me if I'd like a visitor,' she said tightly. 'And I told her I'd rather not.'

'Did you?' The woman looked genuinely surprised and Cathy wondered if she really was as guileless as she appeared, or if this was all part of an elaborate charade.

But the last thing Cathy wanted to do was tread on her feelings. It could have been an honest mistake, after all.

'I'm pleased you came,' she said. 'But won't your Mrs Matthews be wondering where you are right now?'

'I can always call in on Mrs Matthews on my way out,' the woman explained then. 'She usually falls asleep while I'm with her, anyway, which should give you some idea of how boring I am!' She chuckled.

'It's not unheard of for me to visit her and have her remain asleep all the time! That's why I thought . . . but never mind.

'My name's Ellen, by the way — Ellen Atkins.'

'Cathy Galliani,' Cathy supplied, warming to the seemingly absent-minded woman, despite her vague annoyance.

'Galliani? What an unusual name.'

'My husband is . . . ' Cathy took a deep breath, realising it was a slip she would often make at first, 'was Italian.'

'It's hard to think of them as a 'was'

instead of an 'is' at first, isn't it?' Ellen said sympathetically. 'But how interesting — did you live in Italy?'

'No,' Cathy said. 'We lived here.'

'I see. So, how are you feeling? I don't actually know what's happened to you, so it's difficult for me to say whether you look well or not.'

Ellen frowned thoughtfully, then added, 'If you see what I mean!'

'I — we were in a road accident outside Naples.'

And, before she realised what was happening, Cathy found herself opening up to Ellen, who proved to be a very good listener.

Ellen's attention never wavered as she listened, nodding occasionally, smiling along with Cathy sometimes.

'Well,' she said when Cathy had told most of her story, 'I expect you'll be looking forward to getting back with the children?'

Cathy turned her head away, wondering if she had said too much to this woman, who was, after all, a stranger.

'I'm so sorry. Did I mis-understand you, dear?' Ellen's voice was anguished, her face lined with concern, which Cathy inherently knew was heartfelt and genuine. 'I thought the children were all right?'

'I'm not allowed to see them,' Cathy said brokenly. 'They have to remain in Naples with my late husband's family and I must never see or speak to them again.'

Ellen gasped. 'What!' she exclaimed. 'Why, that's disgraceful. It can't be right!

'Surely no-one would be so heart-less . . . ' Ellen's voice tailed off.

Cathy could see that her visitor was shocked by the action of the Galliani family, but what more could she do. Cathy wondered, than offer sympathy and consoling words?

'It's so wrong,' Ellen protested helplessly.

'I know.' Cathy said, 'but what can I do? There was a man here. He brought me this.'

She showed Ellen the open locket with the children's pictures, before putting it back round her neck. 'He found it after the accident. I thought that *he* might . . . But realistically there isn't anyone who can do anything.'

'They're just lovely,' Ellen said hoarsely, then picked up the handbag that had been lying at her feet and began rummaging through it.

'I've got some pictures of my brood here,' she explained.

'My boys!' She laughed, handing the snaps to Cathy. 'Grown men, both of them now. They were only lads when those snaps were taken, though.'

Cathy looked at the pictures and smiled. 'They're very handsome,' she said and Ellen beamed proudly.

'I should have one of my daughter here somewhere, too.' She rooted out another photograph and handed it to Cathy.

Cathy looked at the photograph, a more recent one, and saw a face she immediately recognised. It was Susan, the nurse who had been so kind!

She had been deceived — in the nicest possible way — she was sure of it now, but what did it matter?

Ellen was a warm, funny woman and Cathy felt better for having talked to her. She was a reminder of everything good and normal in an upturned world.

'I couldn't bear it if I didn't see the children again,' Cathy burst out, her eyes bright with longing. 'I love them both so very much.'

'I know, dear. I know.' Ellen patted her hand gently. 'And I'm sure you'll see them again.'

Her voice was filled with conviction as she went on, 'Any woman, anywhere, will know that youngsters belong with their mother.'

'Excuse me, Mrs Atkins, I'm sorry to interrupt you.' A nurse came in. 'But I must ask you to leave now. It's almost lunch time and Mrs Galliani must rest as she's starting physiotherapy tomorrow.'

'I'd like to come and see you again, Cathy, if I may,' Ellen said as she stood to leave. 'I've enjoyed our chat.'

'I'd like that,' Cathy replied truthfully.

The following day was disappointing. Cathy was wheeled down to the physiotherapy unit in a chair and, once there, hardly seemed to do anything at all.

The exercises she did seemed pointless, but she got on with them anyway, trying to put in more effort than was asked of her.

When the session was over, too quickly as far as Cathy was concerned, the physiotherapist wheeled her back to her room.

She hadn't been back in her room long when the door opened — and Vittorio's former boss, Malcolm Edgar, walked cautiously in.

He didn't like hospitals, she knew that much — they brought back unhappy memories of his late wife, Vera's, last illness — and she appreciated all the more the effort it must have taken him to come at all.

'Cathy, my dear.' He clasped her

hand in his. 'What can I say?'

'It's so good to see you, Malcolm,' she said sincerely.

'I've been before, but you were always unconscious,' Malcolm told her, smiling gently.

Malcolm owned two hotels, one of which he managed, the other having been Vittorio's responsibility.

They'd been more than boss and employee, though, more even than friends, and Cathy knew Malcolm had been devastated by Vittorio's death.

'It's really kind of you to come,' she said softly.

'Kind!' He sat down beside her bed. 'It's the very least I could do. When I think back to all the good times the three of us had together! And our outings with the kids, too.

'You and Vittorio were like family to me — it wasn't just the good times, though.

'When I remember how you and Vittorio helped me when Vera died, I . . . I just can't believe Vittorio's gone . . .'

Malcolm's voice faded away brokenly.

Cathy patted his hand consolingly as he sought to regain his composure. But she was too choked to say anything at first.

Gradually, though, she forced herself to say calmly, 'I guess we're both going to miss him for a very long time to come. At least we've still got each other — and our memories.'

She smiled weakly at him and he nodded slowly.

'I heard about the children,' he said softly and the tears suddenly welled up in Cathy's eyes. 'If there's anything I can do to help . . . You know you've only got to ask, Cathy.'

'Thank you, Malcolm. I know you mean what you say.'

Cathy closed her eyes then. She suddenly felt so tired.

'I'd better go now,' Malcolm's words were already a long way off and, at last, the welcome darkness bathed her in sleep.

The weeks dragged drearily by and

Cathy found she was constantly disappointed with her progress.

'You can't rush things,' she was told more than once.

And she'd always reply, 'But I haven't the time to wait.'

Ellen visited almost daily and Malcolm called in as often as he could.

Dan Kirby called in, too, and, while he never stayed longer than a few minutes, his visits were regular. He always seemed to be in a hurry to leave, as if he lived to a strict schedule.

★ ★ ★

Some weeks after the initial sessions in physiotherapy, Dan arrived at the hospital to find Cathy's room empty.

He was, as usual, pressed for time, but he wanted to see her even if it was just for a short while.

He was gradually gaining her trust, her confidence and, in order to maintain it, he had to keep in regular touch with her.

'Can I help you, Mr Kirby?'

He swung round and saw the ward sister approaching.

'If you must see her, then I'm sure it will be perfectly in order for you to go down to the physiotherapy unit — as long as you don't interfere.

'From what I gather, Mrs Galliani is making excellent progress.'

'That's good news,' he said. 'Thank you, Sister.'

She watched as he hurried down the corridor.

A staff nurse had come from the main ward and was now standing next to the sister.

'That young man has certainly been a tonic to Mrs Galliani,' the sister said.

'She was telling me that every time he visits, he brings her books or pictures of Italy and that, in some small way, it made her feel closer to her late husband and children again.

'The poor woman. If it wasn't for him, I doubt if she'd have even that small comfort . . .'

Dan followed the signs to the physiotherapy unit and quietly entered a door which led into a large room, equipped with rubber mats, cushions, weights and several walking aids.

He had never seen anything like it and, to his mind, it looked like a torture chamber.

He was surprised to see Cathy standing up, supported by a walking rail, a therapist on either side.

On her face was a look of grim determination.

Silently, he slipped into a chair at the edge of the room.

'It's enough that you can stand,' one of the women was saying. 'You needn't go any further today, Cathy.'

'I want to,' she said grimly.

'Very well! But don't push yourself too hard.'

Cathy moved off slowly and painfully.

Her movements were jerky and uneven, but the look on her face was a sight to see.

Dan had intended to see her, say

hello and leave. But, as she took one slow step after another, he found it impossible to move.

About halfway along, she stopped and hung her head, exhausted.

Dan moved forward then, into her line of vision. She looked at him, unsmiling, her expression determined.

She'd complained to him many times about seemingly pointless and frustrating exercises she had to endure daily.

But this long, long walk was the culmination of all that effort.

This was the point she had been striving so hard to reach — yet it looked like it was still beyond her grasp.

'Come on, Cathy,' he urged quietly, his whole body tense.

She looked straight at him, seeing him as a link between her and the children in Italy.

She reached to touch the locket, before placing her hand back on the bar.

'I know you can do it,' he said. 'Come on, Cathy.'

She began to move again, slowly and

more steadily, towards Dan, willing herself on.

'You're doing great,' he enthused.

By the time she reached the end of the rails, her whole body was shaking and weak, but it was a triumphant woman who gladly fell into Dan's waiting arms.

'I did it!' she cried happily.

'Did you see me?' she said. 'I walked . . . I actually walked.'

'You were great,' Dan whispered. 'Really terrific.'

In all the tension and uncertainty, he suddenly realised he had forgotten the time. He looked at his watch and was alarmed at just how much time had passed since he came into the hospital.

Getting involved just now had been wrong, he reminded himself. He should have remained an observer — on the sidelines — but he knew that would have been impossible.

It was just as well, he told himself, drawing back further, that he recognised the pitfalls.

To her, he was merely a friend who'd already done her one good turn and who could fill her in on the background of a country she desperately wanted to know.

Dan said a hurried goodbye and left the hospital. He drove as quickly as the traffic would allow. For, on the other side of London, a man was waiting for his report . . .

★ ★ ★

By the end of that week, Cathy was getting about with a walking frame, managing the short distance between her room and the day-room along the corridor.

She felt so much better now, especially as the doctors were actually talking about letting her go home.

She was concentrating on walking when she was startled by the sound of footsteps hurrying towards her. She looked up and saw Dan approaching.

'You're looking good,' he said, noting

the touch of colour in her cheeks and the fact that she no longer looked so thin and frail.

He walked with her to the day-room and they found it empty.

They sat down in opposite chairs.

Immediately, he pulled some photographs from his jacket pocket.

'I've just had them developed,' he explained. 'I took them the last time I was in Italy.'

Greedily, she studied them, her eyes absorbing every minute detail.

'You know,' she said at last, handing the pictures back, 'you don't look like an art historian.'

'Oh.' He smiled. 'And just what are art historians supposed to look like?'

'Pale, from spending hours in dark, ancient places, and bespectacled from peering at all those historic objects by torchlight.'

He laughed aloud and she felt a little silly, but at the time it had occurred to her, it had seemed a valid argument.

'In fact,' she went on, a tone of

annoyance in her voice now, 'I don't know anything about you at all, yet you know all there is to know about me.

'I don't know if you're married, if you have children, where you live . . . '

He looked straight into her eyes.

'I'm not married, I have no children and I live in a flat, a very *small* flat, in the East End of London.'

'I'm sorry,' she said then. 'It's getting close to my discharge date and I'm a bit strung up. I can't believe I'll soon be going home.'

'It's perfectly understandable,' he said. Then, standing up, he added, 'I must go. Here, you may as well keep the photos.

'You still have my number if you need me?'

'Where are you rushing off to now?'

'Another lecture . . . about Queen Hatshepsut's mortuary chapel, would you believe! There are some interesting paintings . . . ' He broke off.

'But I'm talking about Egypt now and you aren't really interested, are you?' He smiled at Cathy, gave a brief salute of farewell and headed for the door.

As he left, Ellen hurried in.

'You're going home soon, I hear,' she remarked cheerily.

'I'm scared, Ellen,' Cathy said tremulously. 'It's been so long . . . I'm really scared. It's so silly, isn't it?'

'There's no need to be scared, love.' Ellen sat down beside Cathy and put her arm around her shoulders.

'I'll do all I can to help. You won't be on your own. And I don't just mean a social worker and physio checking your progress. I'm going to pop in to see you at home whenever I can.

'And there's Vittorio's boss, too. Didn't you tell me he's been like a father to you?'

'Malcolm Edgar? Yes . . . he's been so kind, so supportive. I know he misses Vittorio and the children as much as I do. Actually, he's going to drive me home.'

Cathy felt her former fear evaporating and her old enthusiasm bubbling back.

'Everyone's been so very kind to me,' she said at last. 'You, too, Ellen. I just don't know how to thank you.'

When at last the day came for her to be discharged, Cathy was greeted first by Ellen carrying a suitcase and her knitting bag, then by Malcolm.

She was sitting on the bed, dressed in the clothes Malcolm had brought for her from Oakslee, her and Vittorio's home, feeling very strange.

She put it down to having lived in pyjamas and nightdresses for so long.

'Malcolm!' She struggled to her feet when he arrived. 'This is Ellen. I've already explained to you all that she has done for me.'

'Yes, I remember. I'm very pleased to meet you, Ellen.' Malcolm shook her hand vigorously. 'And I can't tell you how much I appreciate all that you've done for Cathy. She's a marvellous girl!'

Cathy fell silent, happy to leave all the talking to Ellen and Malcolm, who seemed to be getting along well.

While Malcolm went for the car,

Cathy said her goodbyes to the staff and felt sad and happy at the same time.

As Ellen pushed her along the corridor in the wheelchair towards the exit, Cathy spotted a familiar figure. It was Ellen's daughter, Susan, just coming on duty.

The girl spotted her, too, and her face broke into a big smile when she saw Cathy and her mother.

'Hello there, Cathy! Hi, Mum!'

Cathy ignored the greeting and with her arms crossed and a look of mock severity on her face, called out, 'I'm glad I saw you — I've got a bone to pick with you!'

'Me?' Susan's face was a picture of innocence and Ellen was trying hard to stifle a giggle.

'The two of you should be ashamed of yourselves — taking advantage of a poor, defenceless woman and cooking up that scheme between you!

'Still, I'm very glad that you did, now! I'm lucky to have two such good friends — and, Susan, your patients are lucky to have someone who cares so much for them! Thank you again.'

'You're very welcome.' Susan smiled at her warmly. 'Now, off you go — and just concentrate on getting better!

'I'll see you on Saturday, OK, Mum?'

Ellen patted her daughter's arm fondly. 'See you then, Susan. And don't worry about this young lady — I'll be keeping an eye on her . . . '

Outside, the wheelchair taken away by a porter, Cathy walked with the aid of a stick towards Malcolm's car and paused beside it for a moment.

She hadn't realised until now how frightening getting back into a car was going to be, or how many painful memories it would evoke.

'I'll sit in the back,' she said shakily. 'You go in the front, Ellen.'

To Cathy, the journey seemed to take forever, but Malcolm was a competent, careful driver and she began to relax at last, remembering all the uneventful car journeys she had undertaken before the accident.

At last, the car swung into the shady, rutted lane which would take them to Oakslee and Cathy sat up, watching out of the window as the familiar surroundings reached out to welcome her.

When she'd last been here, with Vittorio and the children, the woods had been lush and green, with no signs of acorns and chestnuts.

But now, the leaves were burnished in autumn shades.

She'd missed out on a whole season there and so, she realised had the children!

This time last year, she thought, I was trudging through those woods in my wellies, searching for conkers.

Ellen looked at Cathy, who leaned forward, ready to share her thoughts with Malcolm and Ellen.

'Last time we came down here, we were on our way to the airport.

'I never dreamed then that we wouldn't all come home together.'

Malcolm and Ellen exchanged looks.

There was no bitterness or self-pity in the statement, just a plainly-spoken truth.

Suddenly, the rickety sign for Oakslee was in front of them and Malcolm pulled over close to the hedge.

Cathy stared up at the house, drawing in her breath sharply. It looked so ordinary. Outwardly, nothing had changed.

'I've seen to it that the place was kept tidy.' Malcolm coughed and looked away.

Coming here must be hurting him, too, Cathy suddenly realised. He had his memories as well.

The white walls, touched with moss in places, beckoned as if calling her home.

For a split second, she wondered if she had been dreaming the past weeks. Had it all happened to someone else and she had been told of it?

The hospital was already a far-distant memory, the accident a blurred nightmare.

Without realising it, she was out of the car the second it stopped and standing at the gate, her hand resting on the dew-damp paintwork.

'Are you all right, dear?' Ellen asked, one red-gloved hand reaching out as if to touch Cathy.

She couldn't speak as a tide of memories, mostly sweet, washed over her.

After a moment, she took a deep, shuddering breath. 'I'd like to go in alone, Ellen . . . Malcolm . . . if you wouldn't mind.'

She turned to look at Ellen, her eyes so full of sorrow that it pained the older woman to see it.

'I understand, dear,' she said, drawing away and pulling Malcolm with her. 'I felt the same way after John died. We'll see you later. Just take your time, Cathy. You need time to . . . '

To what? There wasn't a name to put to the laying of ghosts — and Cathy had *three* of them!

She walked slowly up the path, using

the stick the hospital had given her.

When she reached the front door, she opened it and turned to wave at Malcolm and Ellen standing by the gate, looking just like anxious parents.

Then, taking a deep breath, she entered the dark hall and closed the door tightly behind her.

For a moment, she stood there, shivering in the large, empty hall.

The stairs loomed ahead of her and she could almost see Stefano sliding down the banister and landing in a heap at her feet.

She put down her small case and walked through to the kitchen at the back of the house. It was exactly as she'd left it.

The large, stripped pine table was completely clear and her houseplants stood in the sink.

The fridge door was open and she automatically closed it and switched it back on.

She hadn't realised how unnaturally quiet the house was until the fridge began to hum, then it sounded too loud in a house of mourning.

She switched the heating system on and it, too, gurgled into life, adding to the noise.

But anything was better than the deafening silence which had greeted her.

She turned and another, almost visual memory, hit her.

It was Paolina at the kitchen table, her sleeves rolled up, an over-sized apron tied around her waist, her black hair speckled white with flour.

Cathy sank on to a stool for a moment and took a few deep breaths.

She had to get on with the business of living in the present; nothing would be gained by dwelling on the past.

Getting up and moving slowly around the ground floor, she found the house both familiar and alien.

At first, she put it down to the absence of the children, for it had never been a peaceful house — not since she had taken it on anyway.

But something else was wrong here — something that had nothing to do with the silence — that she couldn't quite put her finger on. And it niggled.

Trying her best to shake off her feelings of unease, she picked up the pile of mail which someone, presumably Malcolm, had left for her on the hall table.

She sifted through it, tossing aside the junk mail and putting to one side bank statements, bills and charge accounts.

She was left with a white, foolscap envelope, bearing the name of Vittorio's London solicitors.

Her heart lurched and she began to shake as she carried it through to Vittorio's study, the one room she had been deliberately avoiding.

There was so much of his personality in this room, with its rows of treasured books, the prized desk he had bought for a ridiculous price at an auction and the ornate cigar box which had been a gift from Malcolm.

She sat down in his leather chair and picked up the ivory-handled letter knife to slit open the envelope.

If this letter was what she thought it was, then perhaps getting the children back was not such a forlorn hope. Her heart raced as she removed the contents from the envelope.

The letter was brief. It informed her that the house was now hers and a sum of money would be deposited in her bank account on behalf of the executor of the will, Signor Marco Galliani.

Cathy did a double-take. There must have been a mistake.

The only Gallianis mentioned in Vittorio's will, she was sure, were herself, Paolina and Stefano.

And Marco was not the executor — *she was!*

She reached for the telephone, then decided to check the copy will first.

Only then did she suddenly notice what was wrong — there were *no* photographs in the room!

The framed wedding pictures, the school portraits of Paolina, the studio pictures of Stefano . . . They were *all* gone!

She went through to the drawing-room, as quickly as she could, tapping the parquet floor angrily with her stick as she passed through the hall.

There were no photographs on the piano, either.

Back in Vittorio's study, she was almost afraid to open the safe. But, when she did, her small amount of jewellery and silverware were still inside.

All that was missing were the documents Vittorio always kept so safely — marriage and birth certificates, the children's vaccination and medical cards . . . all were gone.

But why? *Who* would want to take such things — things only of value to her?

Shaking, she sat back down at the desk and half-heartedly opened the bank statement.

A large amount of money had been

deposited in her account quite recently, she noticed.

She reached again for the phone, but changed her mind.

Would the police be interested in the theft of a few photographs? Or a marriage certificate she no longer needed?

She bit her lip nervously. How could anyone be so cruel as to steal her memories!

Looking back now, she found it hard to Visualise Vittorio's face and even the children were impossible to recall clearly.

She could remember little bits of them — their eyes, hair, Paolina's gappy smile. Stefano's chubby hands . . .

Holding the locket tightly in her palm, she realised just how precious it was. For, without it, she would have nothing.

For a moment, she buried her face in her hands, swamped by the enormity of it all.

It was a nightmare, a never-ending

nightmare, and there wasn't a person alive who could help her.

And that was the worst part of all, knowing that she was quite alone and no-one who had the power to change things was on her side.

# 3

Cathy awoke early the following morning, partly because it felt so strange to be waking up in her own bed again.

She wondered if Ellen had slept well. She didn't live that far away and, though Ellen had offered to stay with Cathy for a while, she felt she'd imposed on Ellen's kindness long enough.

Ellen had been a tower of strength throughout these past terrible weeks and Cathy would always be in her debt.

But, Cathy reasoned, Ellen had her own life to lead, her daughter's interests to concern her — and a demanding job helping others. No, Cathy thought firmly, Ellen had done enough already.

So, reluctantly, Ellen had left with Malcolm, who was going to drive her home.

Now, Cathy's thoughts drifted again to the will and the mystery of the missing photographs. Who would want to steal a collection of family photos, Cathy kept asking herself? What use would they be to anyone?

She didn't want to inform the police, though — what could they do, anyway — because she just couldn't face any more upset just now. But she couldn't shake off a vague, uneasy feeling that something more sinister than just a sick note was behind it.

But she was determined to force these worries, for the time being, to the back of her mind.

Today, there was so much to do. The first thing was to sort out the ridiculous mistake concerning Vittorio's will.

The more she thought about it, the more convinced she became that there had been some kind of misunderstanding.

She telephoned Ellen as soon as she was dressed to reassure her that she was coping on her own, then quickly dialled the number of Vittorio's London solicitors.

The earliest appointment the receptionist could give her was for the following morning to see a Miss Redmayne, so she used the time to settle herself back into Oakslee.

She waited in for the district nurse, then took a leisurely stroll in the woods.

Today she would gather her thoughts, tomorrow she would begin to sort out her life.

When the next day dawned, Cathy's mind was buzzing with her impending meeting with Miss Redmayne. By the time the taxi she'd ordered dropped her in High Holborn, she was tired and trembling for she still hadn't worked out exactly what she was going to say.

So many times lately, she had thought, if only Vittorio was here, he'd know what to do. Then the cruel irony of her notion would hit her hard . . .

Taking a deep breath, she walked into the building housing Vittorio's lawyers.

She felt self-conscious and out of place as the receptionist turned to look at her.

'Good morning,' the girl said, her tone friendly. 'Can I help you?'

'I've an appointment with Miss Redmayne,' Cathy said, glancing nervously around. 'My name is Mrs Galliani.'

'Would you like to take a seat?' The receptionist smiled. 'I'll tell her you're here.'

At that moment, a tall, slim woman came in with a bundle of files and set them down on the reception desk.

'Has my appointment turned up yet, Tracey?' she asked. 'I was held up at Gallaghers.'

'Mrs Galliani?' The girl nodded in Cathy's direction. 'She's sitting over there.'

'Ah, Mrs Galliani.' Miss Redmayne extended her hand and Cathy got shakily to her feet. 'Would you like to come this way? I hope you haven't been waiting too long!'

Cathy followed her along a narrow corridor and up a winding staircase into a large, airy office.

'Do sit down,' she said, closing the door behind Cathy. She sat down at her desk and cleared a large pile of files to one side.

'Now, then,' she began. 'What can I do for you?'

'My husband made out his will with you,' Cathy explained. 'He showed me the copy, naming me as executrix . . . '

She paused — she was remembering how upset she had been when Vittorio showed her — she hadn't wanted to think about her husband's mortality — and how he had laughed at her.

'I received this letter from your firm.' She handed the letter over the desk and waited while Miss Redmayne read through it, a frown creasing her forehead.

'This letter is from our Mr Sullivan,' she pointed out after reading it.

'Yes, I know,' Cathy said. 'I just wanted to check . . . you see, my husband definitely made a will naming me as guardian of the children.'

'Children? I see. But I'm sure Mr

Sullivan wouldn't have made a mistake.' Miss Redmayne sighed.

'Someone, somewhere has,' Cathy said defiantly. 'I'm not even allowed to see the children.'

'How awful,' the lawyer said sympathetically. 'I must say, this all sounds very unjust, not to say odd. Look I'll just give Mr Sullivan a buzz. Perhaps he'll be able to shed some light on all this.'

She picked up the telephone on her desk and spoke briefly with her colleague. Seconds later, an adjoining door opened and a small, plump man hurried in, his red face looking decidedly weary.

'I'll take over now, Miss Redmayne, thank you,' he said quickly and, before his colleague could answer, turned to Cathy and asked, 'Would you like to come with me, Mrs Galliani? I'm Martin Sullivan, by the way.'

With this, he turned and hurried out.

With some difficulty, Cathy followed him as he walked swiftly along the corridor into another office. Brusquely, he asked her to sit down.

'Didn't you receive our letter?' he demanded. 'I'm sure everything was set out quite clearly,' he added in an off-hand tone.

He opened a thin file and pulled out a document, studying it again silently.

'Yes, it was, but . . . '

'Then what is your problem, Mrs Galliani?' he interrupted shortly.

Cathy felt flustered, but she hadn't come all this way to be fobbed off or intimidated.

'My husband and I discussed his will before he came to see you,' she insisted. 'He named *me* as executrix and guardian to his children.'

'You're being well provided for financially.' Martin Sullivan glanced at the copy of the will in front of him. 'In fact, I'd say it was an extremely generous settlement. I really can't see what your problem is.'

'I don't care about the money,' Cathy cried furiously. 'I'm concerned with the welfare of the children.'

'As I recall, Mrs Galliani,' he went on coldly, relentlessly, 'the children are *not* your concern!'

'Not my concern!' Cathy exploded, her heart thundering deafeningly in her ears. 'Look, Vittorio wanted me to take care of them — *me*, not anyone else!

'Why on earth would he have gone to all the trouble of making a will if he was intending to change it? I know all about it because he showed me the copy you sent him!

'And that.' She pointed to the document in his hand. 'Is that it? The will?'

'The original is in our strong-room.' The solicitor's eyes quickly slid away from Cathy's and he seemed almost to falter. 'But this copy you mentioned . . . do you have it?'

'No.' She shook her head.

'Look.' He suddenly stood up, so that he was looking down on her. His face was tight, his eyes cold as he said in a controlled voice, 'Don't fight this. Take my word for it, the way things are, you just wouldn't stand a chance.'

The tone of his voice told Cathy that she would get no further with him.

'I think this whole thing is despicable,' she hissed angrily. 'The children belong here with me. Vittorio wanted it that way and, whatever you say, I think you know it.'

Turning abruptly, she stormed out, her fury giving her the push she badly needed now to keep on walking.

Behind her, she heard the solicitor's final appeal. 'Take my advice, Mrs Galliani . . . forget the children!'

The corridor was long and dark and seemed to sway ahead of her as she moved along it.

Wave after wave of dizziness suddenly swept over her and she was inches from the stairs when her knees went weak, as if her legs had no substance.

She reached out for the banister rail, but, before she could grab it as a support, her legs gave way beneath her and she fell to the floor, crying out in alarm as she did so.

Miss Redmayne, startled by the sudden noise outside her office door, hurried to investigate. She was taken aback at the sight of Cathy struggling painfully to get up.

'Oh, my goodness.' She crouched down beside Cathy. 'Are you ill? Whatever has happened?'

Cathy could barely speak, her mouth was so dry, her heart racing. She wasn't even sure if she'd momentarily blacked out.

'I'll call an ambulance.' Miss Redmayne made to rush off but Cathy held her back.

'No, please,' she whispered weakly, 'not necessary . . . I'll be all right in a moment . . .'

'You don't look all right.' She helped Cathy raise her head a little. 'I thought you looked unwell in my office. You certainly can't be left alone in this state. Is there someone I could call for you?'

Cathy considered for a moment, then suddenly remembered the scribbled telephone number in her bag.

'I know.' She struggled up farther to a sitting position and reached for her bag. 'Dan Kirby . . . it's a London number . . . he may be able to come.'

'I'll ask one of the girls to call him.' The woman smiled. 'But, first, let's get you out of the hallway. Do you think you can make it into my office?'

★  ★  ★

Dan was sitting at a large table with two other men, his shirtsleeves rolled up, his tie loosened.

A stack of large black-and-white photographs were spread on the table before them and they were in the process of sorting them.

Another man passing the desk paused and looked over Dan's shoulder. He whistled softly.

'So, that's *the* Galliani,' he said, pointing a finger at Marco.

Dan nodded.

'And that, I take it, is the wife of the younger one?' he went on, pointing to Cathy. In the picture, she was stepping out of a taxi, aided by her husband, outside the Dorchester Hotel.

'Yes,' Dan replied shortly and singled out that picture from the rest.

She looked so different there, he thought, her hair swept up elegantly, her eyes sparkling as she looked almost directly into the hidden camera.

More pictures, taken later, showed Cathy being embraced by Marco Galliani as she and her husband left the hotel. She still looked radiant, relaxed, almost self-assured . . .

'Dan . . . Dan. Call for you . . . '

Abruptly shaken from his reverie, Dan looked across the table at one of his colleagues. He'd been so lost in his thoughts he hadn't even been aware of the telephone ringing.

His colleague was clasping the receiver, his hand blocking off the mouthpiece. 'It's her,' he whispered urgently.

Dan snatched the telephone. The girl

on the line was not Cathy, but speaking on behalf of some city solicitors.

Cathy Galliani, she said, had been taken ill and needed someone to look after her.

Despite what he told himself as he grabbed his coat from the back of his chair, he was pleased for not one, but two reasons, that she had chosen to call him — and only one of those reasons was professional!

'I've got to go out,' he told the other men at the table. 'Tell the boss this is urgent and I'll be back in plenty of time for the meeting.'

By the time Dan Kirby reached the address he had been given, Cathy was sitting downstairs in the reception area, sipping a cup of tea.

'Mr Kirby?' A tall, attractive woman greeted him. 'I'm Lynda Redmayne. I'm glad you're here. Mrs Galliani isn't at all well. In fact, she collapsed right outside my office.'

'Thanks for looking after her. She's just come out of hospital, you see,' he explained with a smile and hurried over to where Cathy waited.

'Hello,' he said gently and, when she looked up at him, he saw the relief in her eyes. 'What are you doing here all on your own, love? Are you all right now?'

She looked away, unable to answer. She felt confused . . . and so helpless. She'd promised Vittorio she would look after the children if anything happened to him — and she was making such a mess of it. Somehow, she felt she was letting him down badly.

Yet she had been so sure of herself at first, so certain things would be easily resolved once she had pointed out the errors. Had she been too naive?

'I thought these people had made a mistake with my husband's will,' she said, her voice cold. 'But it appears I was the one who was mistaken.'

'Come along now,' he said, helping her to her feet. 'Let's get you home and you can tell me all about it.'

She didn't speak at all in the car and

Dan realised, when he tried to make small talk, to crack the ice, she wasn't really listening.

Her mind was obviously elsewhere — probably in Italy.

He parked his car outside Oakslee and opened Cathy's door for her, putting his arm around her to help her along the path.

'Here we are,' Dan said, when they finally reached the house. He'd taken the key from Cathy's trembling fingers and was unlocking the door.

'I'll make some coffee,' he said, once inside, sitting her down on the drawing-room sofa. 'Will you be all right here?'

'Yes, thank you.' Her smile was rather faint, but he hurried through to the kitchen.

Cathy leaned back wearily, her thoughts in turmoil.

She listened to Dan in the kitchen, rattling cups and whistling, and found his presence oddly comforting.

Again and again, the same question went through her mind. *Why* had

Vittorio changed his will?

He must have had a good reason for doing it! Cathy tried hard to remember. When Marco had been in London, Vittorio had seen him several times on business following that first meeting, after which he would return home edgy and irritable . . . almost guilty, somehow.

That *had* to have something to do with it — there was no other explanation. Surely, though, Marco couldn't have forced Vittorio to change his will against his wishes?

He'd been so nice and seemed to genuinely like her. Had she failed some kind of test? Did the Gallianis not think her a suitable guardian for the children? Had Marco sown seeds of doubt in Vittorio's mind about her suitability as a parent?

As always when she was low, her fingers strayed to the locket and she opened it to look at the two faces she loved. Paolina and Stefano — what were they doing now?

The tears she had been holding back for too long began to spill down her cheeks now, blurring her vision of the children's faces.

Dan was now on his way in at that moment, carrying a tray with two cups of coffee and a plate of biscuits. He set it down quickly on the large coffee table and sat down beside Cathy on the long sofa.

'Come on now, Cathy,' he said gently, putting his arm around her silently-heaving shoulders.

He was shocked at the weakness of her body as she sagged against him. Despite himself, he touched the softness of her hair.

Brokenly, she told him about the will, giving him the facts, watching as his expression grew more and more angry.

For just a moment, he saw her for what she was — a lone woman in trouble, with only a couple of friends to turn to.

Every part of him cried out, wanting to help her, wanting to do something to ease her pain other than just watch, helplessly, from the sidelines. But his professional judgment repeatedly told him *not* to get emotionally involved.

Yet, just listening to her heart-broken sobs, seeing the hopelessness in her eyes, sometimes made him wish he'd never taken on this job. And what would *they* think if they saw him now?

For a split second, he almost forgot who he was and, perhaps, nearly forgot just who she was, too.

'Cathy . . . ' he began, putting his arm protectively round her shoulders, aware once again of her fragility, her . . . femininity.

The sudden ringing of the doorbell jolted him back to his senses and he jumped to his feet.

'I'll get it,' he said, relieved to have a diversion.

Cathy remained where she was, unaware of his recent inner turmoil and the effect she had upon him.

\* \* \*

Malcolm Edgar looked questioningly at Dan, who had answered the doorbell so unexpectedly.

'Where's Cathy?' he asked as he stepped into the panelled hallway.

'I've just brought her home from London,' Dan explained. 'She had a bit of a bad turn at her husband's lawyers' office. Oh, she'll be all right now,' he added quickly, on seeing the older man's expression fill with concern.

'What on earth was she doing in London on her own?' Malcolm asked horrified. 'She only had to say — I would have taken her.

'Ellen was afraid she'd do something like this. I should have insisted Cathy let Ellen stay here. Really we gave in to Cathy too easily.'

But she had wanted to be alone in the house and that, to him, had been perfectly understandable. Besides, the hotel wasn't far away and Ellen lived nearby, too . . . Cathy only had to call.

'Well, it's a good thing you were close at hand to help out,' Malcolm went on, shaking his head. 'I'm very grateful to you for taking care of her.'

The hall clock began to chime, startling both men.

'Look,' Dan said, checking his watch. 'I really have to leave now. I've an important meeting at the British Museum at two.

'I hate to dash off like this, but it's a once-in-a-lifetime opportunity and the professor in charge is only there today. It's absolutely crucial I don't miss it.'

'Off you go then.' Malcolm smiled and touched Dan's shoulder. 'I'll take care of Cathy now. Thanks for all your help.'

'Say goodbye to her for me, would you?' Dan said, hurrying towards the door. 'Explain I was in a hurry.'

He was running away and despised himself for being so weak. He knew he had the time to say goodbye to her properly, but he was afraid — afraid of himself!

Malcolm closed the door behind Dan, then hurried through to the drawing room, where Cathy was standing by the french windows looking out over the garden.

'Oh, Malcolm, it's you. How nice to see you.'

'Well, what have you been up to?' Malcolm asked without preamble, his tone mildly chastising. 'Are you feeling any better now?'

'I'm fine now, really.' She smiled, then, looking beyond him, added, 'Where's Dan?'

'He's gone,' Malcolm explained. 'He was in a tremendous hurry, some meeting or other. Talking of meetings,' he added awkwardly, 'would you mind if I use your phone?'

'Of course not.'

'I have to call Ellen, you see.' He looked away. 'We were supposed to be meeting for lunch but I'll telephone the restaurant and leave a message for her. Obviously, I'll have to cancel . . . '

'You'll do no such thing!' Cathy cried, taking the telephone from him and placing it firmly down. 'You can't stand her up! Anyway, how long has this been going on, Malcolm?' she asked impishly. 'You are a dark horse, aren't you?

'Look, you go and meet Ellen — I won't have you spoiling your plans on my account. I really had no idea that you two . . . ' She stopped and winked teasingly.

Malcolm flushed. 'I like Ellen, we get along well. She's a very special, caring woman, Cathy,' he confided. 'To be perfectly frank, I haven't got along so well with anyone since . . . well, since Vera died.'

'I'm glad for you, Malcolm,' Cathy said, regretting teasing him previously. But she couldn't resist adding mischievously, 'Do I detect romance in the air?'

'Well,' he drew himself up to his full height, 'she does seem to enjoy my company as much as I do hers and she's promised to knit me an aran sweater . . . '

He smiled, before adding more seriously, 'But that's by the by. I'm not leaving you on your own like this.'

'Oh, nonsense! Please go, Malcolm,' she said quickly. 'I'll be all right, really I will. If you stay, I'll only feel obliged to be a perfect hostess.'

He had been through such a lot over the last few years, it was about time life dealt him a winning hand and Cathy couldn't think of anyone better than Ellen.

Vera, his late wife, had been his life and to lose both Vittorio and Vivianna so soon after her death was no less than tragic.

'I don't know.' He hesitated.

'I'm very tired,' she said, knowing she'd convinced him. 'I'd like to have a nap, so you really should go. Now, please hurry, you mustn't keep Ellen waiting. I hope you both have a nice time.'

When Malcolm arrived at the restaurant, he looked around for a moment before seeing Ellen but, as he hurried over to their table, he smiled warmly at her.

'I'm sorry I'm so late, Ellen,' he said, taking the seat opposite hers.

He went on to explain about Cathy.

'Poor thing,' Ellen sympathised. 'It's a good job Dan was available.'

'Yes,' Martin agreed. 'He seems like a good sort — ' Then he broke off. For, coming out of a doorway on the other side of the road, was Dan himself. Yet he had told Martin he had an unmissable meeting at the British Museum at two. It was that time now — and the Museum was miles away.

Dan was obviously lying — but why?

Malcolm looked out of the window again, but Dan had gone, melted away. There was something funny going on and he hadn't a clue what it was.

He liked the man, yes — there was nothing about him to dislike! But he no longer trusted him.

⋆ ⋆ ⋆

Cathy yawned and stretched. She hadn't meant to fall asleep on the sofa, but had been too shattered to bother with the stairs.

How she despised the weakness which still ruled her life and how she looked forward to the day when she would be her old self again!

As always, her waking thoughts turned immediately to the children. If only she could see them again, talk to them, reassure them! They wouldn't know how much she missed them, or how determined she was to get them back where they belonged.

They would think that she had forgotten them!

She stood up, her legs stiff, and moved to the window.

A light breeze ruffled through the fading shrubs and the double swing in the garden creaked emptily — the bare, muddy patch beneath it had already healed without the devastating invasion of small feet every day.

A red and white football rolled around in the kitchen garden. It was Stefano's ball, the one Vittorio had always fretted would go through his greenhouse.

'Stefano, Paolina,' she whispered, wanting to hear their names out loud, to reaffirm that somewhere they still existed. She clenched the locket in her fist. 'I would do anything to have you home with me. *Anything!*'

The house cried out for them and the garden was strange without youthful laughter.

The telephone bell jangled and she snatched it up quickly to stop the intrusive sound. It was the district nurse, reminding her that she would be calling again the next day.

'I'd forgotten,' Cathy admitted ruefully.

'That's understandable.' The nurse was surprisingly kind. 'You've a lot on your mind right now, but you must put yourself first.'

After she'd hung up, Cathy held the telephone in her hand, the germ of an idea forming. She couldn't see the children and any letters she wrote would probably never be passed on.

But, if she were to call them . . . Surely, they couldn't object to her enquiring after the children?

She didn't put the phone down, but dialled international directory enquiries for the Gallianis' telephone number — it was so easy!

As soon as she had it written down in front of her, she dialled the number and was amazed to hear the telephone ringing at the other end after only a brief pause and a few clicks.

Yet, it seemed an eternity before someone answered at the other end.

There was a slight pause, then, 'Hello?'

She didn't realise at first that the voice which spoke to her was English, or even vaguely familiar. It was so unexpected.

Her chest tightened and she could hardly breathe.

She was all geared up to speak to one of the Gallianis, ready to plead, argue, whatever it took, but this . . . this she realised, was a child.

'Hello,' she finally blurted out, 'who is this?'

There was a further moment's hesitation on the line, then a loud sigh which sounded almost like a sob.

And, in that instant, Cathy *knew*, without doubt, who had answered the telephone.

'Paolina!' she cried, as tears of joy began to course down her face. 'Paolina, darling, is that you?'

'It's me,' the child cried, joy and sorrow choking her small voice. 'It's me. Oh, Mummy . . . Mummy!'

# 4

Cathy clung tightly to the telephone, almost as if she could keep hold of Paolina herself as long as she didn't let go.

She couldn't understand a thing the child was saying at first, as her words were tumbling out in a long, garbled rush — Paolina was so like her father when she got upset.

'Slow down, Paolina,' she said, her voice calm, belying how she really felt. 'Take it easy, darling. Tell me how you and Stefano are getting on. How is . . . '

'I'm frightened!' Paolina cried, her voice shaking. 'Stefano's having horrible dreams again and he cries a lot and . . . and he doesn't speak much, Mummy.

'Every night he wakes up, calling for you, but you never come . . . We miss you, Mummy.' There was the mildest hint of accusation in her voice and Cathy felt her face flare red-hot with shame.

'Don't you love us any more?' Paolina burst out. 'We want to come home. We want you . . . Don't you feel well? Is that why we can't come home?'

'Paolina, I — I'm so sorry, darling. I *do* love you both and I want you home with me, but — '

'Mummy, please, we just want to come home. Please!' Paolina said, her voice small and lost at the other end of the line.

Cathy was about to say more when she heard a man's voice, then there was a slight pause before the sounds of a scuffle and Paolina's shouts of protest at the other end as someone wrested the receiver from her hand.

'Paolina! Paolina! What's going on?'

'This is Silvano Galliani. Who are you?'

The voice was cold, dignified and utterly chilling as if the owner of it was quite detached.

When she listened hard, she could still hear the sound of Paolina's sobbing noisily in the background.

'It's Cathy . . . Cathy Galliani. Oh, signore, I just wanted to speak to the children, to check — '

'Listen to me,' he interrupted with such authority that Cathy fell silent. 'You have upset my granddaughter with your call.

'Forget the children. They are our grandchildren, Marianna's and mine. They are nothing to do with you. They are my son's children. They belong here, with their family — not with you.'

Losing her temper would solve nothing, but still Cathy had to force herself to sound reasonable.

'Signore . . . ' she began, but the line clicked as he hung up before she'd had the chance to utter another word.

For a long time she held the receiver, staring at it incredulously, listening to the uncompromising burr of the dialling tone. She felt choked and terribly hurt.

Trembling all over, she put the phone down. The children needed her as much, if not more now, than she needed them — that decided it! She had made up her mind.

* * *

Far away in Italy, it was raining steadily, Silvano Galliani was staring out of the window, watching the rain trickling down the panes, his fingers still on the cut-off buttons of the telephone.

With a deep, troubled sigh, he released them and replaced the receiver.

He turned then, suddenly feeling the eyes of his own mother boring into his back from the doorway. She'd been such a help looking after the children while Marianna was in hospital for her operation.

Paolina, who had been watching him from a corner of the room, fled, still sobbing, brushing past her great-grandmother, refusing to accept the solace of her arms.

The old woman's eyes were accusing and sharp as she glared at her son. She was small in stature, but she was his mother and he knew only too well how strong and indomitable she really was.

'Are you happy now, Silvano?' She tossed back her head and her mouth tightened into a hard line of scorn. 'I never thought I would see a son of mine being so hard, so unfeeling, for his own flesh and blood. What would their grandmother say if she was here now and not in a hospital bed? She would be appalled to see her little grandchildren so unhappy!'

'It is for the best, Mama,' he said, taking up some papers from the table and pretending to become absorbed in them. His attitude was impassive and this infuriated the old woman.

'For the best! How can you say that?' She turned and held open one of the double doors so that Paolina's weeping could be heard quite clearly. 'Listen to the sobs of the child you profess to love!'

'With respect, Mama, this is not your concern,' he said, walking past her. 'I am doing the right thing, rest assured. And please don't upset Marianna by mentioning this business to her.'

'The right thing for whom, Silvano?' she called after his retreating back. 'For the children . . . or for yourself?'

Fiora Galliani shook her head sadly, then turned towards the stairs. This was her concern. She might be old and frail, but she still knew right from wrong.

With one hand on the ornate banister rail, she walked up the stairs as quickly as she could, following the wailing to the nursery.

It was the same nursery which had been Vittorio's.

She went in and looked around. Everything a child could ever want was in that room — toys, electronic games she couldn't begin to understand, a beautiful giant rocking horse — but the children left them all untouched.

Stefano wanted nothing but his precious Toppolino, a stuffed mouse his stepmother had given him, and Paolina just seemed to sit all day.

Fiora sighed deeply. Paolina had pretty dresses, Stefano could have anything his heart desired, but the one thing they really needed was a mother.

So what if Cathy was not their natural parent? It didn't seem to make any difference to the way they felt about her. Paolina was sitting on Stefano's bed, her thin brown arms wrapped around him as they both cried so bitterly and loudly.

They looked so small, huddled together. Fiora hurried over to the bed, sat between them and took them both in her arms. They loved her and clung tightly to her warm body.

Damn Silvano! His stubborn family pride! Children should never know such unhappiness, she thought fiercely.

She looked up over their heads through a haze of tears and saw Silvano watching her from the doorway, his dark eyes troubled, a frown creasing his uneven features.

The tears vanished from her eyes as she spoke. Her voice was low, tinged with a venom he hadn't heard from her lips in years.

'Can't you see what you're doing? For pity's sake, Silvano, look at them.'

'Blood is blood,' he said thickly, holding her gaze defiantly. Then, turning abruptly, he hurried away.

★   ★   ★

Dan Kirby wiped a patch of condensation from his window and looked out pensively.

It was a grey day out there, damp and misty, and it seemed to match his mood. He knew the reason for his melancholy.

Hadn't he lain awake half the night again, thinking of Cathy Galliani? The woman haunted him, asleep or awake. He found it impossible not to think of her lately — the way she walked, her uncertain smile and the light in her eyes whenever she spoke of her beloved little family . . .

He admired her courage as well as her femininity and there was no denying that she was a very attractive young woman.

She was mature beyond her years, yet so vulnerable.

No matter how hard he tried, he could not forget how it had felt to hold her in his arms, albeit for such a brief time.

It was several days since he had taken her home from London and he missed seeing her. He moved back from the window, letting the curtain drop. His flat in the Docklands was smart, if a little functional, but it suited him.

Pouring himself a coffee, he pondered his feelings. They were so unprofessional, and it was unusual for him to allow himself to become emotionally involved.

It was getting even harder to remain detached when he was with her. But there were forces at work here, within him, even he didn't understand.

He wanted to ask her out, but . . . but

*nothing!* Why *shouldn't* he? He couldn't help the way he felt about her.

The telephone rang and he picked it up, his voice brisk. 'Kirby here.'

'Dan? Hello, am I calling you at a bad time?'

Immediately, his voice softened. 'Cathy,' he said warmly. She sounded brighter, more alive than when he'd last seen her.

How odd that she had chosen this moment to ring — the very moment he had been thinking so deeply about her.

'Dan? Are you still there?'

'Sorry,' he replied steadily. 'It's good to hear from you. Actually, I was just thinking about you. How do you feel?'

'Fine, thanks,' she said jovially. 'In fact, I'd like to see you . . . I've something important to tell you. Are you free tomorrow?'

'Yes,' he answered, puzzled over the reason for her sudden elation.

'Could we meet for lunch?'

'Why not make a day of it?' he suggested impulsively, as a sudden madness caught hold of him. 'We're in for some fine weather, I'm told. We could spend the day at Hampton Court Palace — ever been there?'

'No,' she replied. 'But it sounds lovely. Are you sure you don't mind?'

'Mind! Of course not,' he said. 'What time shall I pick you up?'

'No, don't come here,' she said quickly, the first hint of unease in her voice. 'I — I'd rather we kept this between ourselves for the moment. Let's meet at the palace itself — say, ten o'clock?'

'I'll look forward to that, Cathy,' he said. 'See you then.'

It wasn't until after he had put the phone down that it occurred to him that his boss mightn't approve.

With a broad smile, as he lifted his coffee cup to his lips, he realised he couldn't care less!

\* \* \*

Cathy was standing looking over the river, a light breeze ruffling her hair.

Her face was flushed and she looked so alive, so vital that Dan could hardly believe she was the same woman he had last seen on the point of collapse.

This ridiculous infatuation of his was becoming embarrassing. It was so preposterous, not to mention utterly foolish, on his part to entertain any such feelings.

She had been deeply in love with her husband — that had always been more than obvious to him — and, if she were to discover the depth of his feelings for her now . . . the consequences would be unthinkable.

Suddenly, as if she sensed his presence, she turned and her hair blew in a curtain across her face so that she had to brush it away with her hand.

'Dan!' She smiled.

'You're early,' he said.

'So are you.'

'You said you had something to tell me.' He spoke fast, wanting to get the business out of the way first.

'I called Italy a few days ago,' she

began to tell him, 'and I actually spoke to Paolina. She's desperately unhappy, Dan, and little Stefano, well, he's hardly saying a word.

'I've got to get them back before any more damage is done.'

He nodded, knowing there was more to come — she hadn't asked to meet him just for that. She looked directly at him, her eyes dark and intense, and put her hand lightly on his arm.

'I'm going to Italy, Dan. I've made up my mind,' she told him firmly. 'I've spent all week arranging it — the hotel, the flight, everything. I've even seen my doctor and the district nurse and they wholeheartedly approve of me getting some sun!

'I've been to the bank and sorted out my money and . . . well, it's all fixed. I'm so much fitter now and I don't think I'll ever be as ready for this trip as I am now.'

She was staring at him, pleading with her eyes for his understanding, waiting for his reaction. But she found it impossible to read the expression on his face.

'Are you quite sure you're up to it?' he asked eventually.

'I've never been so sure of anything in my life,' she said calmly. 'Don't you see, Dan? I no longer have any choice. The children need me.'

'I can understand that,' he said. 'So, when are you leaving?'

'Tomorrow!'

'So soon?' It was impossible for him to hide his surprise and she smiled, pleased to have said something at last which caught him off guard.

'It's all arranged, but . . . ' She paused and tightened her grip on his arm. 'Dan, I have to ask you a favour. I hope you don't mind.'

'Go ahead!' He grinned.

'I want you to call Malcolm for me, but not until after ten o'clock. I'll be on my way by then and he and Ellen won't be able to stop me.'

She released his arm and shrugged her shoulders — a gesture she had unwittingly picked up from her late husband.

'You know what they're like — they'll only worry about me. Reassure Malcolm for me; tell him I know what I'm doing.'

'They wouldn't approve,' Dan observed wryly.

'Certainly not. When I told them of my intentions, they were so upset . . . I had to let them believe they'd talked me out of going. Anyway, would you do this for me?'

'Is that *all* you want me to do?' he asked.

'It's very important to me,' she told him simply.

For a second, he let his hand cover hers, then a party of schoolchildren suddenly rushed past, knocking Cathy off balance so that Dan had to hold on to her to stop her falling over.

'Kids!' he said in exasperation, more to cover his own turbulent feelings than anything else.

'They make the world go round.' She

laughed, yet her smile was wistful as she watched the children running away, pursued by a worried teacher.

Much later, as he drove home, Dan made a detour to his office. For a while today, he had allowed himself to relax and enjoy the company of a lovely woman. Now his mood was grim.

The boss would have to be told of the latest developments, there was no getting away from it, but would he approve of what Dan wanted to do . . . ?

★　★　★

Malcolm Edgar was halfway across the hotel foyer when Carol, the receptionist, called him.

'Telephone for you, Mr Edgar.'

'I'll take it here,' he said and hurried into his office, closing the door firmly behind him.

'Malcolm Edgar,' he said, sitting down as he picked up the receiver.

'Good morning.' The voice was

familiar. 'This is Dan . . . Dan Kirby.'

'Mr Kirby?' Malcolm's back straightened and his eyes narrowed. 'What can I do for you?'

'I have a message for you,' Dan said. 'From Cathy.'

'A message? From Cathy?' Malcolm said, baffled.

'She's on her way to Naples at this moment. She took a flight this morning.'

'She did *what?*' Malcolm bellowed, standing up and knocking his chair flying backwards.

'Naples! And you knew about it? For pity's sake, man, how could you let her go? You know how delicate her health is!'

'I'm sorry, but she was determined,' Dan said quickly. 'If I'd tried to stop her, well, she would simply have gone behind my back, too.

'At least this way we know what's going on,' Dan said, a slight undertone of reproach in his voice which made Malcolm bristle.

'But she doesn't know Naples at all. She's hardly travelled anywhere in her life.'

Malcolm righted his chair with his right hand and sat down again, pressing his thumb and forefinger into the top of his nose. 'Frankly, Dan, I'm very worried about her.'

'Look, don't worry too much. I was due to go out to Italy again soon and I've been able to bring my trip forward a few weeks.

'I should be able to keep an eye on her — from a distance, of course.'

Malcolm put the receiver down and stared blankly at his desk. Off to Italy, just like *that*! And Cathy, how could she have been so rash?

\* \* \*

The sun was shining when Cathy's plane landed at Capodichino Airport and, as she disembarked, a gentle breeze, warm and welcoming, wafted into her face.

She hurried with the rest of the passengers through customs, with a hesitant smile playing on her lips.

She felt so happy to be there, despite the bitter memories which would always be inextricably entwined with Italy.

She felt good, here at last on the same soil as the children.

'Signorina.' A driver jumped out. He was already pulling open the door of his cab with one hand and grabbing for her case with the other.

'You want a taxi, si?'

'Thank you, yes.' She was startled by his enthusiasm.

'Welcome to Italia.' He put her case in the boot, then ran around to the driver's door.

'Where to, lady?' He grinned, his teeth a white block against the darkness of his skin. 'I am at your disposal.'

'This hotel.' She handed him a piece of paper.

He revved the engine and roared off down the road at great speed, chatting animatedly and pointing out the various sights to her.

Cathy looked about her — under different circumstances there were many things she would have liked to see while she was here. But, this time, her visit had only one purpose . . .

At last, the car stopped outside a small hotel. Cathy was beginning to feel tired and too hot.

'Here we are.' The driver turned around and leaned over his seat, handing her a small, printed card. 'For you, signorina. My telephone number. Call me, wherever you want to go, whenever. Day or night.

'Ask for Gino, si? I have the radio in my car and I know all the best places to see.'

As she took the card, he saw her plain gold wedding ring and was at once contrite. 'I am so sorry — signora!'

'That's all right, Gino. Thank you.'

'I leave you now.' He gave a short bow. 'Enjoy your stay and remember to call Gino if you need a cab.'

Her large, air-conditioned room was cool and she thankfully sat down on the bed for a moment, wiping her forehead.

Her eyes felt heavy and, suddenly, she felt the urgent need to lie down and, before she knew what was happening, she had fallen into a deep, exhausted sleep.

When she awoke some time later, she felt refreshed, if a little crumpled, and got up to unpack her case.

After a late dinner, she showered and went to bed, too excited, too full of her own thoughts, even to open the book she had brought from home.

In the morning when she awoke she realised that she had just had her best night's sleep for weeks and was feeling a little more sure of herself, if that was possible.

Today, she would go to the Villa Felicia, confront Vittorio's parents and see the children.

After breakfast, she checked that her appearance was all it could be then went into the foyer and dialled the number Gino had given her.

He was there within 10 minutes.

'I've written the address down,' she said, handing him a piece of paper on which she had printed the address of the Villa Felicia.

'No problem!' He grinned, then, as his eyes scanned the paper she had given him, they darkened like coals.

'Are you sure you want this address?' he said, frowning.

'Yes. Why? Is something wrong?'

'Nothing is wrong,' he said, but made no attempt to start the car. His radio crackled and a voice spoke to him in rapid Italian.

Cathy didn't understand all Italian, especially when it was being spoken quickly, but she had become used to Vittorio's Neapolitan accent and knew enough to translate what the operator was saying.

'Gino, your wife telephoned,' the speaker on the other end of the line began. 'She said you're not to forget to pick up the laundry today!'

Gino acknowledged the call and Cathy smiled broadly at him as his whole attitude changed — he was relaxed and friendly again.

It must all have been in her mind. Obviously there was nothing to worry about.

She was about to make some comment about the call, but his next words took the wind right out of her sails, leaving her sitting there with her mouth open in dumb surprise.

'Ah, I am so sorry, signora,' he said, spreading his hands. 'I apologise most deeply, but I cannot take you anywhere today.

'My wife, she is very sick, you understand. That is what the radio message was about. I have to go to her at once.'

Cathy stared at him, perplexed. What on earth was he talking about?

'I'm sorry, you will have to call another taxi.' He got out and opened the door, then stood impatiently waiting for her, as if he couldn't get her out of his car quickly enough.

She stared at him, stupefied, unable to speak, to protest.

'I'm sorry,' he repeated, without looking at her.

She got out obediently, realising she would gain nothing by arguing, and stood on the pavement watching as he sped away.

*Why* had he lied? Why was he friendly and sparkling one moment and next . . . well, he was little short of hostile?

She bit her lip, wondering what to do next. What had she said to provoke such a reaction?

Looking back, she couldn't think of a single thing. In fact, all she had done was to hand him an address — the address of Villa Felicia!

# 5

Cathy watched until Gino's little car was swallowed up by the rest of the traffic. She still couldn't believe what had just happened to her!

The message which had come over Gino's radio had been quite innocuous, yet the way he'd reacted anyone would think . . . and why did he find it necessary to lie?

With a deep sigh and a resigned shake of her head, she made her way back into the hotel, momentarily defeated. She had been all psyched up and now this set-back had rather knocked her for six.

What else could she do? Was it possible that no cab would be willing to take her to the villa?

'Scusi, signora.' The girl polishing the reception desk looked over at Cathy with huge dark eyes which were a startling and unexpected reminder of Paolina. 'You have a . . . em . . . problema?'

'I can't seem to get a taxi,' Cathy replied slowly in Italian. 'I had hoped to go visiting this morning, but now . . . ' She shrugged hopelessly.

The girl also shrugged, then reached under the desk. 'You drive? You can hire a car from Signore Pace — he's very cheap. I have his number.'

'Thanks.' Cathy took the printed paper. 'I hadn't thought of hiring a car, but I don't see why not. I'll need a map, too.'

'We have maps.' The girl smiled as she produced a bundle of leaflets. 'Napoli, Salerno, the islands. Take whichever you need, there's no charge.'

Cathy selected just one and thanked the girl again; then, with the printed paper clutched tightly in her hand, she hurried over to the pay-phone to contact the car hire firm.

The car was outside the hotel within 15 minutes, its driver a thin, balding man with eyes like jet and a perpetual smile on his thin lips.

He spoke remarkably good English and Cathy was relieved. She still found speaking constantly in Italian a strain.

'I will sit beside you and you can drop me at my office,' he told her. 'It will give you time enough to become acquainted with the car. I used to drive in London . . . lots of hooting and shouting!' He laughed. 'Just like here.'

She was grateful for the short practice drive. The left-hand drive, coupled with the difference in the Neapolitan traffic, was nerve racking.

After she'd dropped Signore Pace back at his office, Cathy opened her map and started marking her route with a red pen.

Soon, she was driving out of the city and quickly found herself on a long, dusty road which took her closer still to Mount Vesuvius.

The road wound and twisted, narrowing down to a car's width in many places.

So, this was where Vittorio had spent his childhood!

She passed through a tiny crop of uneven dwellings, with white, stucco walls topped with faded red roofs.

The place was hardly big enough to be called a village, but Cathy was fascinated by the scene and stopped the car. She could go no farther than this anyway without asking someone for directions.

She called out to one of the women selecting fruit from a stall which was fixed to the back of a wagon. 'Mi scusi, signora. Dove posso trovare la Villa Felicia?'

The woman came over to the car, speaking in rapid Italian as she did so. But Cathy caught and understood most of what was said.

'Grazie, signora.' Cathy smiled warmly at the woman, before slipping the car into gear and driving away.

As she left, she looked in the rear-view mirror and saw two men coming from one of the black-arched doorways.

They appeared to question the woman Cathy had spoken to and she was aware of them watching her until she had driven out of sight.

The Villa Felicia was close now and her heart began to hammer, whether with fear or excitement, she couldn't be sure.

The track turned a corner, widened and ended abruptly at a high, white wall, which was partly hidden by palm trees and bushes laden with heavy, colourful blossoms.

She turned the car and stopped directly in front of two high, black, iron gates. The words, *Villa Felicia*, were wrought into the intricate pattern of the gates.

'This is it,' she told herself, licking her lips nervously before getting out of the car. She smoothed down her clothes, ran her fingers through her hair and walked shakily to the gates.

She felt small and insignificant and couldn't help shuddering a little in the face of the unknown.

*. . . I was only allowed to leave the villa to attend church . . .* Vittorio's words echoed in her mind now.

Her heart was pounding unevenly, for it had suddenly hit her — she was here at last! She had made it to the Villa Felicia!

A faint click startled her and she looked up to see a small, compact video camera following her movements, the tiny, red light watching like a single eye.

Unnerved by the camera, she stood against the gates, winding her fingers through the cool iron as she looked in.

She shivered. It was so beautiful and grand, but all this tight security created the wrong environment in which to raise young children, especially when they were used to running free the way hers were.

She turned and pressed the intercom button which was at eye level, trying to ignore the presence of the whirring camera above her head.

'My name is Cathy Galliani,' she said, surprising herself with the firmness and sureness of her own voice. 'I've come to see the children.'

She had expected something, though she wasn't sure what, but not the long, ominous silence that followed.

Someone was there, watching her, listening to her, yet they chose to hide behind their electronic gadgetry.

'I won't leave until I've seen the children,' she repeated determinedly, angered by the silence. She stepped back from the gates and looked directly into the camera lens, unafraid now, as renewed determination took over.

'Please,' she went on. 'Just let me have a few minutes with the children.'

She stared at the camera, demanding a reply and, as she stared, the red light snapped out and she realised no-one was watching or listening any more . . .

* * *

Behind a large, modern desk, surrounded by shelves crammed with papers and books, sat Silvano Galliani.

His finger had just depressed the shut-off button on the camera unit, leaving the screen to return to its former blank, green state.

Behind him, small and dark, stood his mother, Fiora, a deep scowl etched into her lined face. She had been watching Cathy, too, with keen interest, seeing her expression change from determination, to desperation, to fury.

She had also seen the love, the hurt and the anxiety for the children which darkened the young woman's eyes. It was genuine love, she suspected, not the possessive kind Silvano knew.

Her heart went out to Cathy and she knew, more than ever before, that the children belonged with Cathy, their mother, as is every child's right.

'Why did you do that, Silvano?' she demanded coldly. 'You were wrong to spurn that young woman, very, very wrong. You saw her, didn't you? You saw how upset and worried she was.

'At least, open the gates and speak with her — have the courage to tell her to her face why she is being separated from the children she loves.'

Silvano swung round in his seat and stared up at his mother. 'How can you accuse me of lacking courage? Will you never give up, Mama?' he shouted angrily.

'I have told you time and time again, my mind is made up. The children stay here!'

He got to his feet and stood towering over his mother, his face red with anger.

Fiora stood her ground, but she was shocked and hurt at his outburst.

'How dare you! How dare you speak to your mother in that way, Silvano,' she said, her voice shaking with indignation. 'I'm still your mother and you'll remember that and treat me with respect.'

'I apologise, Mama.' He looked away, guilt written all over his face. 'This business is harrowing for us all and the sooner that woman gives up, the better for everyone.'

'Ah, you are so wrong, mi figlio.'

Fiora smiled, her dark eyes creasing. 'She will not give up. Did you not see the look in her eyes? Can you still remain so blind to the truth?'

'What can I do? What can I say to convince you, Mama?' Silvano went on desperately, his eyes tortured. 'I'm acting in the best interests of my grandchildren, for Vittorio's sake.'

He sighed loudly. 'It would seem I have no alternative but to tell you the whole truth. Enzo, the file on the Englishman, please.'

A short man, who had been sitting dispassionately witnessing the argument from his seat in the corner, jumped to his feet and immediately fetched a thick folder which he handed to Fiora with a respectful smile and a short bow.

'What is this?' She held the file in her hands.

'There is a man, Mama, called Daniel Kirby. You may remember that he was the first to arrive at the scene of the accident.'

'Yes, yes, I remember,' Fiora said

impatiently. 'The kind Englishman who called the ambulance. Paolina said he sang to her while they waited for help to arrive.'

'Kind Englishman!' Silvano sneered. 'We have been watching him for months. He poses as an art historian . . . No, take the file for yourself, Mama.

'Read the truth about how kind this man really is, then come back to me and tell me that you still believe my son's children belong with that woman!'

Fiora made her way unsteadily to her bedroom, her thoughts in turmoil. Surely she couldn't have been mistaken all this time?

Alone in her room, she closed the door and walked over to the writing desk in the corner, where she sat down, put on her glasses and opened the file.

Within a clear, plastic folder was a large, coloured photograph of Daniel Kirby and, stapled to it, a note about his profession. She gasped. No, it couldn't be. La Guardia!

There followed pages of text detailing

his visits to Cathy in hospital and afterwards. So, he was a policeman. She fanned herself with one of the pages — there was even a picture of him as a very young man in uniform.

The evidence was all there in front of Fiora. He had had the Gallianis under surveillance for some time, even being there for Marco's last trip to London.

She pressed her lips together in a tight line. So, maybe he didn't care about the girl after all. Maybe it *wasn't* such a coincidence that he was on the road immediately after the car crash had happened, after all.

And Cathy, Vittorio's widow, what part did she play in all this? Was she working with this policeman in some way, wanting to take the children in order to get at the Gallianis?

She shut the file and took off her glasses, laying them down on her desk.

She was an old woman and whatever the file said, she knew Vittorio would never have fallen in love with Cathy if she hadn't been sincere and genuine.

For she had seen real love in Cathy's eyes. And she had never had reason to mistrust her own instincts in the past.

Vittorio would tell the truth — he had never lied to her.

She pulled a chain from around her neck and removed a small key which she used to unlock the top drawer of her desk.

Inside, bundled together neatly and tied with a blue ribbon, was a stack of letters. Lovingly, she ran her gnarled fingers over them, her eyes filling with stinging tears, as she recalled her grandson's last day with her before leaving for England.

'Remember Vittorio, I love you and, while it breaks my heart to say goodbye to you, I am proud of you for what you're doing.

'It takes a strong man indeed to stand up to your father and Uncle Marco. It's hard for them to understand you want to make it on your own.

'I'm glad you understand, Nonna.' Vittorio had hugged her warmly. 'I hate leaving you, but I'm going to make a good life for us in England — a good, honest life.'

With hands that now shook, she undid the ribbon and removed the first letter from the pile.

Cara Piccola Nonna Fiora. She smiled and a tear trickled down her dark, weathered face. Dear Little Grandmother Fiora. He had called her by that pet name since he was 13 years old and already taller than her.

She read through the rest of that letter and, in the quiet room, it was as if Vittorio was with her, speaking to her, laughing in that carefree way of his.

His uncle's way was not his and that was a blessing.

*My boss, Malcolm Edgar, is such a kind man. He's been so good to us and his wife, Vera, is a great friend to Viviana. The baby will soon be here, Nonna, and we are so excited . . .*

She read through each of the letters in turn, unfolding them with great care and tenderness. Each one brought news, first of Paolina's happy birth and later another pregnancy, then of Vittorio's great sadness at the death of the kind Englishwoman called Vera.

Then, so soon, another letter had come, this one bringing such tragic news that even now it brought a rush of tears to Fiora's eyes.

*. . . I have heard today that Viviana is ill, Nonna, but refuses to have treatment until the baby's born. The doctors say that, by then, it will be too late. But she will not risk the baby. I don't know what Paolina and I will do without her . . .*

There was a long space of time then between letters and, from the next one Fiora opened, there fell a small snapshot of a tiny baby, his eyes screwed up and his lips pursed.

She put the photograph down gently and opened the accompanying letter *. . . Viviana died this morning, Nonna. I feel absolutely devastated. Paolina is inconsolable and the baby . . . I wish you were here with us, Nonna. I don't* *know what to do.*

*Every time I look at Stefano, I'm reminded of the sacrifice his mother made and I'm overcome with guilt and grief.*

*I love the baby but I can't bear to hold him yet.*

Poor child, Fiora mused, born with no mother to love him and a father too shocked and confused to care properly.

Then, then he should have come home to the bosom of his family. Then, the children would have accepted life in Italy, but now, it was too late.

*. . . Cathy is so lovely, Nonna. She looked after me in hospital and now I see her often. I had forgotten what it was to be happy until now. She reminds me of you . . .*

*I want to marry her and I know that you will be glad.*

Fiora smiled. This was what she had been waiting for, the happy letters, the ones which arrived with even greater regularity than before.

Vittorio came back to her in those

letters, as if he had been dead and come alive again.

Eagerly, she opened another letter, then another, before she opened, perhaps for her, the most significant one of all.

*. . . we were married yesterday. It was a quiet wedding and Malcolm and the children were with us.*

*It saddens me that you couldn't be there, but things the way they are between my father and me, it was unavoidable.*

*As you know, I'd been worried that the children wouldn't take to Cathy. I should have known better. Already she is a friend to them. No, Nonna, I do them all an injustice. She is more than that — she is a mother.*

*They love, trust and confide in her and since they have known her, Stefano has started to come out of his shell. Paolina is a different child, too, no longer moody and wilful.*

*Cara Nonna, I have told my Cathy that you will always be there for her, as you have been for me. I've told her that there's no-one in this world she can trust more than you.*

*If you knew her, I know you would love her. She is yours as I am.*

Fiora sniffed and slipped the carefully-folded letter back into its envelope. It was the first time she'd read them since Vittorio had been killed.

When he'd left for England, she'd known she would never see him again, but had always assumed that it would be her own death which would part them for ever . . .

And Cathy had been too ill to attend the funeral. But she should still have been informed of his resting place so that she might pay her own respects.

In this she, Fiora, in abiding by the wishes of Silvano, had failed to live up to Vittorio's words of trust. That, more than anything else, caused her the greatest pain.

She tied the letters together, but did not return them to her drawer. She opened the file again, looked at the clear blue eyes of Dan Kirby and pressed her fingers into her forehead.

What should she do? What could she do?

At last, she reached a decision. Knowing exactly what she must do, she picked up both the file and the letters and hurried downstairs.

Silvano looked up from his desk. 'So? Have you read it?' he said, unable to hide the triumphant gleam in his eye. 'Did you read about the brave guardia?'

'Yes, Silvano, I have read it. Every word,' she said solemnly. 'Now it's your turn to do something for me. I want you to read these!'

She dropped the letters on to his desk in front of him.

'What's this?' Silvano flicked the blue ribbon contemptuously with his fingers. 'I'm busy . . .'

But Fiora had turned her back and was already on her way out of the door.

Impatiently, he scattered the letters across his desk and threw the ribbon aside. It was only when he recognised the large, uneven hand of his only son that he selected a letter at random and opened it.

Since Vittorio's departure, Silvano had received no more than greetings cards from his son and they all bore the same cold, formal messages. Yet this . . . it was hard to believe this newsy, affectionate letter was from the same person.

Why couldn't he write to me like this, he thought sadly. Why did he cut me off? Who is this Malcolm Edgar he writes of so fondly?

*. . . Malcorn and I went fishing last week. It was a great day, Nonna, like a son with his father. I don't think I ever went anywhere with my father — his mind was always so much on the family business. No wonder I grew to regard him as a stranger.*

*Cathy taught Paolina to bake and I have dutifully eaten the results. They are playing with Stefano now and I can hardly think straight for his noisy giggles. It's a sound I never expected to hear.*

*Thank God Cathy has shown me what I've been neglecting for so long.*

Silvano closed his eyes and pushed the desk lamp to one side. He had lost his only son a long time before Vittorio died on the highway.

Always, he had done what he thought was right and when Vittorio had dared to disagree, they had fallen out and Vittorio had chosen to take his wife into exile rather than remain at the villa.

If only he had accepted Vittorio's decisions, then he need never have lost the love of his only son! Feeling suddenly very old and overwhelmed with loneliness, Silvano ran his fingers roughly through his hair.

He was a ruthless man, hardened by years of struggle and the constant fight to stay alive. His own childhood had been hard, living in the slums of Naples in total poverty.

But the day his father was gunned down in the street to lie dying in his older brother, Marco's arms, was the day Silvano had vowed that this would never happen to his own flesh and blood again.

Nothing would ever be allowed to hurt the Gallianis in the future.

He read on, glad that Vittorio had at last learned to show his feelings for his own son. His only regret was that he had learned this lesson not from his own father but from a young Englishwoman . . .

★　★　★

Cathy sat down in the quiet of her room and sipped the tea which had been made specially for her.

The hotel staff were like a family — they'd worried and fussed all over her when she had come back to the hotel, pale and shaking.

When at last she'd managed to convince them that all was well, she'd retreated into the privacy of her room.

She swallowed two pills with her tea, hoping to clear her head, then picked up the telephone and dialled Malcolm's number.

It would have been so easy to break

down and cry. But, to do that now would be to admit defeat — and she wasn't defeated, not by a long chalk!

'Cathy!' Malcolm sounded thrilled to hear her voice and not at all cross as she had feared. 'It's good to hear from you. Are you all right, dear?'

'I'm fine, Malcolm. It's good to hear you, too. It's lovely here — so warm and pretty — and I've seen some of the sights.'

'And the children?' Malcolm asked, for they both knew she had not rushed to Italy for the sightseeing.

'No,' she said quietly, her voice catching. 'I haven't made much progress yet, I'm afraid. How's Ellen? Are you both well?'

'Never mind about us!' Malcolm retorted gently. 'You're the one we're worried about. Remember, you've been ill and you're still supposed to be convalescing. I don't know what your doctor was thinking about, condoning this trip. Why don't you come home?'

'I can't.' She shut her eyes and

wished the pills would begin to work. 'I won't consider coming back until I've at least seen Paolina and Stefano. I'm not going to give up that easily. Have you seen Dan at all?'

'No! He called me.' Malcolm said. 'But I expect you've seen him by now.'

'Seen him? Dan? What are you talking about, Malcolm? How can *I* have seen him?'

'Well, he told me he was going to Naples to look after you.' Malcolm sounded miffed. 'You must have seen him by this time.'

'Of course I haven't!' Now it was her turn to sound annoyed. 'Was this your idea, Malcolm?'

'No, but it isn't a bad one. You know how I feel about you fighting this all on your own. Anything could happen and I'd never forgive myself if you were hurt.'

'I can take care of myself,' she said sharply but without malice. 'Look, Malcolm, give my love to Ellen and please don't worry about me.

'I must go now, I'm going to have a rest. So you see, I *am* looking after myself. You take care, too.'

'Keep in touch,' Malcolm said quickly. 'And send us a postcard.'

★　★　★

While Cathy wandered the streets of Naples, sampling ice-cream and buying gifts, Dan's plane had landed right on time.

It was almost 24 hours since Dan had hurried through passport control, with little time or inclination to notice the atmosphere of the place, or to revel in the warmth of the welcoming sunshine.

He'd joined the small queue waiting for taxis and was delighted when a cab had pulled up right beside him.

'Come with Mario, signore.' The cabbie leaned out of his window. 'Best cab in all Napoli. Best prices.'

Dan jumped in gratefully with an apologetic smile at the disgruntled people who were left to wait.

'Where to, signore?'

Dan reeled off the name of Cathy's hotel, then settled back in his seat to do some serious thinking. He was looking forward, of course, to seeing her, but he'd have to tell her who he was.

He'd have to admit that he worked in New Scotland Yard and that he didn't rub shoulders with professors, but with Customs men and the Italian police.

She would probably be angry, so angry that she would never wish to see or speak to him again, but he owed it to her to tell her of the danger she was in.

She seemed blissfully unaware of the kind of people the Gallianis were, or how close she was to a world of everyday violence and corruption.

The journey was taking an interminably-long time. He glanced out of the window at the unfamiliar scenery and froze.

'Hey!' he shouted. 'What's going on? Is this some kind of short-cut?'

The road was narrow, winding and dusty and he knew perfectly well it would not take him into Naples — they had already left the city far behind.

The driver looked over his shoulder, his eyes dark and narrow. 'Shut up,' he snapped, his English heavily accented. 'You go where Mario say.'

'Just a minute.' Dan sat forward, his pulses racing as adrenalin began to flow through his body.

Putting his hand inside his jacket, he reached for the gun which usually nestled within his shoulder holster, but touched only the cotton fabric of his shirt.

He cursed quietly for he was not wearing his firearm. He would never have made it through airport security with it.

He had never needed the gun before, but now, more than ever before, he wished he had it with him.

He was unarmed — and trapped in the back of a car being driven too fast to who knew where.

His hands scraped along the glass partition between him and the driver, but it was useless — there was no means of opening it from his side.

Angrily, he hammered on the glass, but the driver ignored him. At last, the car skidded into lay-by at the side of the road, sending up a cloud of white dust.

It was a quiet, secluded spot in the middle of nowhere — but Dan was already looking for a way out.

He jumped from the car before the dust had settled and was about to make a break for it, when a long, black limousine pulled up parallel with the vehicle he had just left.

He stopped in his tracks as three men got out and stood silently beside their car. They were all fairly burly. He studied their faces, intending to remember every detail, from their unsmiling lips to their size ten feet.

Stepping back, he realised these men meant business and he was ninety per cent sure that they were armed.

It was no accident that he had been brought here and the reason was of no great surprise to him — it was something he lived with every day of his working life.

There'd always been the chance that, one day, something could go wrong.

'This is it,' he muttered softly to himself, running his tongue over his parched lips.

'Guardia!' The paunchy man in the middle spat and the others took this as a cue to advance slowly.

Dan backed up, looking desperately to his left and right for a means of escape.

One of the men reached into his jacket and pulled a gun and Dan could remain silent no longer.

'Wait a minute,' he said boldly. 'You're making a big mistake here, mate!'

They ignored him and kept on coming until they were only inches away.

It was only then that Dan remembered his way back was blocked by the cabbie . . . As he turned, pain rocketed through his skull, sending a searing shock-wave down his spine before darkness blocked out everything and he felt no more.

# 6

When Cathy had finished speaking to Malcolm on the telephone, she took a quick shower, then went straight to bed.

She fully intended to get up again later, but it had been an exhausting and dispiriting day and her mind and body cried out for rest.

She would probably have slept soundly until morning, had she not been wakened by a persistent knocking at her door. She snatched up her watch from the bedside table. It was well past nine o'clock and dark outside.

'Uno momento,' she cried, tugging on her robe and holding it tightly around her as she padded barefoot to the door.

'Signora!' It was the daughter of the hotel owner. 'Scusi, signora, you must come quick. A policeman is downstairs . . . he wants to speak to you urgently. I think you should come. There has been an accident!'

'An accident,' Cathy repeated, as a wave of dizziness washed over her. Not another accident. 'What has happened? Do you know, signorina?'

The girl shrugged. 'I am sorry, signora. He does not tell me — just to get you quickly.'

Dressing as fast as she could, Cathy hurried downstairs and was startled by the sight of the uniformed policeman waiting for her. Her only hope was that this was a case of mistaken identity.

He approached her as soon as she entered the foyer, bowed gallantly and spoke in clear, precise English.

'Signora Galliani? Signora Cathy Galliani?'

'Yes.' She frowned. 'What's all this about?'

'I apologise, signora, for disturbing your rest, but it is very important that you come to the hospital,' he said. 'You are needed.'

'Needed?' she said. 'Who could

possibly need me? I don't understand.'

'I am sorry. I can't give you details.'

'But surely there's something you can tell me?' she insisted, as she followed him out to the car. 'You must know why I've been sent for!'

He turned to look at her and shrugged. 'I can't tell you what I don't know.'

'Then at least tell me who needs me?'

'I really am sorry.' He smiled. 'I have simply been instructed to bring you to the hospital.'

He opened the car door and, hesitantly, she got in. She sat beside the officer in the back of the car as it sped through the dark streets, her mind racing . . . if anything more had happened to the children . . .

At last, the car stopped outside the hospital and the officer led her inside, hurrying by the reception desk with a brief explanation to the nurse on duty.

They went up in a lift, then along a brightly-lit corridor to a room where another policeman sat outside. He stood up as they approached and exchanged a few words with Cathy's escort.

'This way, please,' the officer said, as he opened the door to a dimly-lit room.

She was in no hurry, scared of what she might find. Haltingly, she entered. The room was full of machinery surrounding a single bed. A small monitor in the corner bleeped with reassuring regularity.

Slowly, her legs feeling like lead, she went over to the bed, pressing her hands hard on the rail at the foot as she peered over the white sheet.

The room began to sway and she had to fight to keep hold of her senses as she saw the person in the bed.

'Dan!' she whispered. 'What happened?'

She turned to look at the policeman, but he did not answer her question.

'You may stay for two minutes,' he said with a look at the attending doctor who now rose and nodded his agreement. 'No more.'

Then he and the doctor turned and walked out of the room, shutting the door behind them and leaving her alone.

Awkwardly, she moved round the bed, then, as she sat down, her nursing instincts automatically took over and she lifted one of his limp hands to hold in her own.

'Don't worry, Dan,' she said. 'I'm here now.'

'Cathy?' he replied, his voice barely audible. 'I'm sorry . . . didn't mean . . .' He tried to rise, but was too weak and slumped back against the pillows, quickly dropping off to sleep again.

Tenderly, she touched his forehead with gentle, cool fingers. 'It's going to be all right, Dan.'

At that moment, a nurse hurried in and smiled apologetically at Cathy.

'Scusi, signora, I must ask you to leave for a moment.'

Very reluctantly, Cathy left the room, her mind whirling in confusion. She'd felt so strange in there. But it wasn't the shock of seeing a friend badly injured. It was something different . . . it was a feeling of warmth and tenderness at seeing Dan — feelings she'd hardly experienced since Vittorio's death.

'Are you all right, signora?' The doctor was hurrying towards her, a look of concern on his face.

'This has obviously been a shock for you,' he went on. 'Would you like to sit for a moment?'

'No, I . . . ' She looked at him, then at the sympathetic face of the policeman. 'I'd like to be told what's going on.'

'This way, please.' The doctor took her and her escort to a room at the other end of the corridor.

Inside, the doctor sat at his desk and motioned Cathy to a chair while the policeman stood near the door.

'Signore Kirby was badly beaten, then shot twice in the chest.' He watched Cathy carefully, gauging her shocked reaction. 'If it had not been for some American tourists who had lost their way, he would be dead.

'They found him at the side of the road and brought him to the hospital. It is a miracle he lives.'

Cathy could only shake her head disbelievingly.

'But why?' She looked up at them. 'Why would anyone want to hurt Dan?'

The two men exchanged glances. 'We have no details at this time,' the policeman said eventually and Cathy got the very strong impression that he was lying . . . or at least not telling the whole truth.

'What are his chances?' She addressed the doctor. 'Can you tell me that?'

'We'll know better in the morning,' he said. 'He has been calling for you since he came round from the last operation some hours ago.

'You probably saw that he is still not fully conscious and we wouldn't expect him to be for at least another six hours.

'As to his chances, signora — if he lives until the dawn, then I believe he will make a full recovery. He is a very strong man.

'But I should warn you, the odds are against him making it through the night.'

Cathy was still reeling from the shock when the policeman spoke again.

'I'll take you back to your hotel now, signora.'

Dan was dying. No, he couldn't be! Not that strong, vital man who'd made her laugh, dried her tears and given her hope. No, it just wasn't fair.

'I'd rather stay,' she said distractedly, 'if that's all right with the doctor. I'll keep out of the way. I used to be a nurse and know how a patient in this condition should be treated.'

The doctor nodded. 'You obviously mean something to him. Of course you may stay. Your presence may prove to be beneficial.'

She hurried back to the room then took her seat beside the bed, once again taking Dan's hand in hers. How the tables have turned, she thought, as she gazed down at him!

A long way away, Ellen looked around her at the sparkling, crystal chandeliers which hung from the ceiling.

Malcolm watched her as she looked around, still awed by her surroundings, almost as if she were a gauche, young girl.

'I've had such a wonderful day,' she said, slightly embarrassed at his unwavering gaze. 'I can't remember when I last had so much fun.'

'I'm glad.' He reached across the table and took her hands in his own. 'It's been a pretty terrific day for me too, Ellen.'

She sighed — a long, happy sound which ended in a smile.

'Oh, Malcolm, don't you wish life was always like this?' She hadn't meant to think aloud and blushed.

'I do . . . and it could,' he said, straightening up slightly, but keeping tight his hold on her hands.

'What? Strolls in beautiful forests, the best play I've ever seen, followed by

161

dinner and dancing at one of the world's finest restaurants?'

'It's more than that . . . ' He spoke quickly now, fearing his courage would fail him. He wanted to put his feelings into words before the moment was lost and his chance with it.

The way he was looking at her now made her shiver with delight.

'I don't want to embarrass you, but I have to say something,' he said. 'When Vera died, I never expected — or wanted — to fall in love again, but I have.

'Ellen, I love you, more than I would ever have thought possible.'

'Malcolm!' She gasped. She couldn't believe it. She had wanted to hear those words from him, wanted to say the same things in return . . .

The love in his eyes intensified, but there was a trace of anxiety there, too, and her heart went out to him.

'It's the same for me, Malcolm. I haven't looked for love either, but it's found me and I'm very, very happy. I love you, too, darling, so very much.'

'Oh, Ellen . . . ' Malcolm whispered, tightening his grip on her hands. 'I was all ready for retirement and a peaceful old age, but now . . . now all I want is to live my life with you.

'I'm asking you to marry me,' he said softly. 'I want you to be my wife.'

The world seemed to stop as a quiet stillness fell. Ellen was so happy and proud she thought she might burst.

'You don't have to give me your answer straightaway,' Malcolm went on, releasing her hands.

'I couldn't keep you waiting,' she said at last, her voice soft. 'I don't have to. My answer is yes, Malcolm.'

'If you need more time to think . . . ' he went on, then suddenly broke off, his face breaking into a happy, relieved smile. 'What did you say?'

'I said, 'yes'.' She smiled.

All at once, he was on his feet and had pulled her into his arms. Two waiters, who had been watching discreetly, averted their eyes politely as two very happy people kissed.

Cathy was almost drifting off to sleep, when Dan's voice, soft and weak, broke through her thoughts. Instantly, she was alert and leaned over to listen.

'I'm here, Dan. It's me, Cathy.'

'Didn't . . . didn't mean to deceive her . . . '

'Who, Dan?'

'No.' His face contorted in some internal anguish that she couldn't reach. 'Cathy, no . . . please . . . she means so much . . . '

'Dan, it's all right.'

'Never . . . never forgive me . . . can't lose her . . . '

The nurse hurried over to the bed and looked down anxiously.

She placed her hand on Cathy's shoulder and smiled. 'I am going for the doctor,' she said. 'Will you be all right here, alone?'

'Yes.' She looked back at Dan. So who was this mystery woman who meant so much?

He was muttering again and she bent

her head closer to hear.

'Cathy . . . Cathy, thank goodness . . . ' His fingers gripped hers, although he didn't open his eyes. 'Don't leave me . . . I don't want to lose you . . . Cathy . . . '

'I'm here, Dan. Don't worry.'

With a shock, Cathy realised that he had been talking about her — she was his mystery woman!

'I'll stay with you, Dan,' she said, her voice trembling.

He fell silent once more and his body became still and peaceful as he slept. The nurse came back with the doctor, and Cathy stood back while they examined him.

The doctor turned to her, smiling. 'It's promising, signora,' he said. 'He's stabilising. I'm going to let the nurse take a break now. The emergency buzzer is just there if you need help.'

She was grateful for the time alone in the room. What Dan had been saying, unreal as it seemed, had touched something deep within her — something she would rather have kept hidden even from herself.

She was surprised that she cared so much, shocked, too.

After all, Vittorio had been dead only a matter of months! How could she feel this way so soon?

'Oh, Vittorio,' she whispered to the air, 'why did you die?'

★ ★ ★

In the morning, the doctor came into the room and examined Dan again. He seemed pleased with his progress.

'Thank you, signora. You being here certainly helped,' he said. 'He's going to pull through.'

Cathy couldn't believe the feeling of joy that coursed through her at the doctor's words.

But, even as he left her alone again with Dan, she couldn't help thinking about who had shot him — and why?

And why was it necessary to have a police guard on his room? Was he still in danger?

But Dan had started to come round now and, when he opened his eyes, he saw her.

'You've been here all night,' he said weakly. 'Thanks, I appreciate it.'

'How did you know?' she asked warily.

'The nurse told me.' He winced with pain. 'I think I knew anyway.'

'I'm going back to the hotel now,' she said. 'I need some rest and to freshen up. I still feel a bit shaky from the accident, sometimes. I'll come and see you later.'

'Cathy . . . '

She stopped and turned back from the door.

'There's something I must tell you.' He was trying to sit up but couldn't make it.

'Not now, Dan. You must rest.' She hurried back and made him lie down again. 'You're still very ill.'

'It's important . . . '

'All right.' She sat down.

'Cathy, I . . . ' He turned away, pain searing across his face. 'I don't know how . . . you won't like it . . . Cathy, I lied to you.'

'What about?'

'I'm a police officer . . . an under-cover police officer.' He shut his eyes. 'I hate myself . . . for having deceived you. You've been under surveillance for months. I've been watching your every move . . . I'm sorry, Cathy.'

For a split second, her heart seemed to stop beating as the meaning of his words sank in. The implications of what he'd just said hit her with tremendous force and she was shocked into stunned silence.

'Say something for pity's sake.' He moaned. 'Don't just sit there looking hurt.'

'What do you expect me to say?' she said. 'I don't know what to think, never mind what to say. Why did you lie, Dan? I thought you were my friend. I really thought you cared — I didn't realise it was all part of your job.'

'I am . . . I do . . . I was just following orders. But, as time passed, I did begin to care.'

'What orders?' she demanded.

'We've been watching the Gallianis . . . they're into organised gambling, among other rackets. When Marco Galliani, the big boss of their operations, came to London to meet Vittorio, we thought they intended to spread their operation to Britain. Then you . . . you became involved.

'Cathy . . . ' He grabbed at her fingers, an agonised expression on his battered face. 'They did this to me — the Gallianis.'

'You can't expect me to believe that,' she said, astounded. 'You're making a big mistake, Vittorio would never . . . '

'I know. We quickly realised he was clean,' he mumbled. 'But listen — take care. They tried to kill me. You could be in danger too.'

She backed away from the bed — the Gallianis were responsible for this? Impossible!

But . . . just before the crash, what had Vittorio been trying to warn her about? He had been so upset, frightened almost, when his uncle came to

London. Suddenly, everything seemed to slot neatly into place. No wonder Vittorio had wanted to be out of it!

The doctor came in just then and touched her shoulder.

'What are you still doing here?' he asked. 'You look exhausted.'

'I'm leaving now.' She smiled wanly, knowing she had to get some rest.

'Try to get some sleep. Will you be back later?'

'Oh, yes.' She looked again at Dan. Despite everything, how could she not come back?

As soon as Cathy got back to the hotel, she called Malcolm. 'I've so much to tell you,' she began. She had almost reached breaking point and needed Malcolm's solid voice to keep her steady.

'It's Dan,' she went on. 'He's turned up.'

'I see.' Malcolm's voice was brittle and suspicious. 'I was wondering when he'd show.'

'He's badly hurt, Malcolm. He's in

hospital. He's been shot.'

'Shot!' Malcolm spluttered. 'Shot?'

'He's not an art historian,' she went on. 'He's an undercover policeman.

'I know this is going to sound incredible, Malcolm, but he's been investigating Vittorio's family . . . '

'Hang on,' Malcolm ordered. 'I can't take this in. It's unbelievable. A policeman, you say? Good grief, I had no idea. I knew there was something odd about the fellow, but . . . are you sure? Can you be certain that he's telling you the truth now?'

'He says the Gallianis tried to kill him,' she replied. 'I have no reason to think he'd make up something like that.'

'I don't know what to say, Cathy. You don't need this on top of everything else, do you? What about the children? Have you heard anything more?'

'No,' she said. 'I've got to keep trying, though. But it's like banging my head against a brick wall, and now I know the kind of people they are . . . it makes my blood run cold.'

'I think you should come home. In view of what's happened, you'd be better off here.'

'I can't do that,' she said. 'How can I leave the children with them now, knowing what kind of people they are?'

'Yes, yes. I understand how you feel. But, for goodness' sake, be careful and, if there is anything, anything at all that we can do . . . '

'Thanks, Malcolm. You and Ellen would be the first people I would come to. Are you both well?'

'We're fine . . . Oh, Lord, I almost forgot.' His voice lightened. 'Last night, I asked Ellen to marry me and she agreed.'

'Oh, that's wonderful,' Cathy cried. 'I'm so happy for both of you. Congratulations. Do give Ellen my love.'

She had never heard Malcolm so happy and could well imagine Ellen's joy. If ever two people were made for each other, those two were.

'I'll do that,' Malcolm replied. 'Take care.'

* * *

Silvano Galliani reclined in a chair, reading a newspaper and smoking a cigar. He was unaware of his mother's approach, and her sudden presence startled him.

Some time had passed since they last had words and an uneasy peace now existed between them. He should have known it was too good to last.

'Well?' she said abruptly. 'You must have read my letters by now. You've had time to think things over. What's your decision?'

'Not now, Mama.' He put his paper down and strode over to the window.

'Don't turn your back on me, Silvano!' Fiora said sharply. 'I'm asking you a simple question. Did you read the letters?'

'I read them,' he said, his voice low.

'Then, surely, you can see it now?'

She hurried over to him and he couldn't fail to recognise the hope in her voice. 'You read Vittorio's words. Can't you see they confirm what I've been telling you all along?

'The children are pining for her — they love her as if she were their own mother. The letters prove it. Enzo checked the hotel for me. It isn't too late, Silvano. She's still in Napoli.'

Silvano looked straight into his mother's eyes — he could see the accusation in them as she regarded him closely, waiting for his reply.

He could put it off no longer. Things couldn't go on as they were.

'What are you going to do, Silvano?' Fiora asked softly. 'I can see in your eyes that you have come to a decision.'

'Yes, Mama.' He turned around and put his cigar to his lips. 'I know exactly what to do — I've known for some time.'

# 7

The doctor was smiling as he looked down at Dan. 'I've heard that you're to be moved this afternoon, for your own safety,' he said.

'Moved! Where?'

'An ambulance and specialist nursing team will take you to the airport and you'll then be flown back to London.'

'How long have I been here?' Dan asked. 'I've lost all track of time.'

'Just a few days.' The doctor grinned. 'Although your visits from the signora must have made the time pass more quickly.'

Cathy had been in to see him every day and every time he saw her, she seemed to have withdrawn a little more into herself. He knew she still wasn't feeling completely well but there was something more behind it — almost as if she was losing her fighting spirit.

Cathy came in at that moment and the doctor quickly excused himself and left.

'How are you?' She looked closely at Dan's bruised face and smiled.

'Fine.' He grinned. 'In fact, I've just heard that I'm to be sent home this afternoon!'

'Today!' She turned away. 'So soon? Are you sure you're ready for that?'

'They say it's risky for me to stay here. Look, Cathy, I want to get things straight between us before I go.

'I'm sorry about how things have worked out,' he said sadly. 'I'd give anything for the situation to be different.'

'So, you're off home then,' Cathy tried to sound brisk.

'Come with me, Cathy,' Dan said impulsively. 'Don't stay here all on your own.'

'I can't do that, Dan.' She looked down at him through a haze of tears. 'I can't go back now. I've been through too much. I won't leave till I have the children back.'

'You must realise what you're up against by now,' he said. 'Your life could be in danger.'

'There must be a way to get Paolina and Stefano.'

'I wish I could help, I really do,' he said miserably, aware of his own weakness. 'But I can't. I know them — I know what kind of people they are. I'm a professional, Cathy, and look where it's got me.

'You've phoned them and even been to the villa and it's got you nowhere.'

'Do you think I don't realise that?' she burst out angrily.

She got up to leave and he realised she probably hadn't listened to a word he said. He cursed the weakness which prevented him getting out of bed and physically stopping her.

'If you won't come back with me,' he said quietly, 'then please be careful'

'I will,' she said. 'I'm glad you're going home, Dan. I don't expect to see you before you go, so good luck.'

'Wait,' he called after her. 'Can I see

you . . . when you get back?' he asked tenatively.

She walked slowly back to the bed. 'You know where I live, Dan.' She leaned over and kissed his forehead. 'You'll always be welcome at Oakslee.'

With that, she turned around and hurried from the room before he could see the fresh tears in her eyes. What hurts most of all was that he was right. For, no matter what she did, it would be a waste of time.

She was beaten!

By the time Cathy got back to her hotel, she had reached the bottom of her own private well of despair. Without the children her life seemed empty and pointless.

When she glanced up, she noticed a black limousine was trailing her as she hurried towards the hotel entrance.

She tried to see in the windows, but it was impossible to see beyond the dark, tinted glass.

She quickened her pace, Dan's warnings coming back to her.

Suddenly, the car overtook her and stopped. Then a man stepped out and stood on the path in front of her, blocking her way.

'Signora Galliani,' he said, 'come with me, please.'

'No.' Her nerves were taut and she backed away, fear wrapping ice-cold fingers around her heart. A hand reached out and touched her arm and she wrenched herself free.

'Don't touch me!' she cried. 'Leave me alone.'

'There's nothing to fear, signora.' The man smiled. 'I will not harm you.'

'Just leave me alone.' Her voice rose and she turned around and began to run back the way she had come.

'Signora, do you wish to see the children?'

She stopped dead in her tracks and whirled around. It could be a trick. She realised that and yet . . .

She was so afraid, her heart was hammering hard.

'I don't believe you,' she said warily.

'If you don't come with me, signora,' he said mockingly, 'then you'll never know the truth.'

She swayed on her feet. Put like that, she had no choice. She had to go with him — it was a risk she had to take.

'Very well,' she said, stepping towards the car, the decision made. 'I'll come. I must see the children.'

'Good!' He grinned and, as he opened the door for her, she couldn't help feeling like a chicken trapped within a fox's den.

★ ★ ★

In no time at all, they came upon a villa, smaller but no less grand than the Villa Felicia, and the car swept through the gates and up a long drive.

'Where are we?' she asked nervously as the car stopped and the driver opened the door for her.

'Go on inside. You are expected.'

Automatically, she got out of the car and walked shakily up the steps and through the open door into a large, cool hall.

Her eyes were still adjusting to the change in light when she saw a small figure beckoning to her from a doorway. 'Cathy . . . I have waited so long to meet you. Do not be afraid, child, no-one will harm you.'

I'd like to believe that, Cathy thought, as she approached the old woman.

'I am Fiora, Vittorio's grandmother.' The woman kissed Cathy on both cheeks. 'Come with me, please.'

Reluctantly, Cathy followed the woman into a large room where Fiora sat down.

'What is this place?' Cathy asked. 'Why have I been brought here?'

'The villa belongs to my elder son, Marco. I believe you and he met when he was in London. The answer to your second question is more complicated.

'My son, Silvano, is not a bad man — he has a heart much like any other. He loves Stefano and Paolina deeply and so do I.'

So, that was it! Fiora was simply

reinforcing the family's stand. They wanted her out of the country and off their consciences and that was what this was all about.

'He is a lonely man,' Fiora went on. 'Vittorio leaving the family as he did caused him great pain and heartache. And later . . . '

'Nonna Fiora,' Cathy began, but Fiora silenced her with a look.

'We haven't much time. It's my belief and my daughter-in-law, Marianna's, too, that a child belongs with its mother. Any woman, anywhere, will agree with that, but a man . . . ' She shrugged. 'For a man, it is harder to understand.

'What is it, child? You have gone quite pale.'

'You've just reminded me . . . someone once said something very similar to me. I . . . I didn't believe her at the time.'

Dear Ellen, how wise she really was!

Fiora smiled knowingly and rang a small bell, then got unsteadily to her feet.

'Marianna and I will miss the children terribly — she was so looking forward to being with them when she came out of hospital — but we both know it must be.'

For a moment, they stood in silence, just looking at each other, before the door flew open — and Paolina and Stefano rushed in!

Stefano hurled himself at Cathy, tightening his arms around her neck so that she could feel the wetness of his tears on her face and taste the salt on her lips as she kissed him.

With her free arm, she clung to the trembling body of Paolina, who held her tightly about the waist.

This was it. The moment she had been longing for, dreaming of, for months. Oh, the joy of holding the children in her arms again. She looked over Stefano's head at Fiora and she saw that she, too, was near to tears.

But now that Cathy had them, she was never going to let them go, no matter what.

From behind a pillar at the far end of the room. Silvano turned away, drawing his hand down his face as if he could wipe away the sudden, unexpected pain he was feeling.

His older brother, Marco, put his arm around his shoulders and drew him silently and unnoticed into another room.

'Oh, Mummy.' Stefano sobbed loudly, still clinging to her neck. Paolina cried quietly, her eyes screwed up tight, as if the pain was too much to bear.

The moment seemed to go on for ever. Yet, it could only have been a second ago that none of this had seemed possible.

Stefano relaxed now, resting his head on her shoulder, a look of contentment on his face. Paolina leaned against her, her eyes big and round in her peaky, worried little face.

'Come along now.' Fiora found her voice at last. 'In here are your tickets and papers. Your flight to England leaves this afternoon.'

She handed a brown envelope to Cathy, then reached for another, bulkier envelope.

'I believe these are yours, too,' she went on, seeming to falter with embarrassment.

When Cathy opened the envelope, she understood why — it contained all the photographs and family papers taken from Oakslee!

'But why?' Cathy said, at last. 'Why are you helping us?'

'It would take too long to explain.' She patted Cathy's shoulder. 'But please don't forget Nonna Fiora!'

Stefano held even tighter to Cathy, but Paolina broke free and hugged her great-grandmother.

'I'll write to you, Nonna,' she promised tearfully. 'I wish you could come . . . '

'Ah, but who would look after my Silvano? He puts on a big, brave face. But, underneath, he needs his mother — just like you!'

'Tell your son,' Cathy broke in

shakily, 'that Vittorio was a good man and I loved him very much.'

'Thank you,' Fiora whispered. 'It means a lot to me and will to him, too. Go, now! Enzo will take you back to your hotel.'

'I don't know how to thank you.' Cathy, tears of happiness shining on her face, embraced the frail old lady. It was over! She didn't have to fight any more.

'Go, go,' Fiora urged. Much more of this and she would break down herself and that would not do at all.

She went into the big hall and watched as Cathy hurried out into the sunshine. Then Fiora's heart suddenly leapt as Cathy turned and ran back, Stefano still in her arms.

Wordlessly, the young Englishwoman slipped the locket she treasured from her neck and gently pressed it into Fiora's hand.

Fiora's fingers tightened around it as she watched Cathy go outside where the joyful voice of Paolina squealed a greeting.

Then the old woman returned to the big room, sat down, lowered her head into her hands and began to cry . . .

'Where are we going, Mummy?' Paolina cried, as Cathy ushered them into the waiting car.

'Home.' She laughed, still unable to believe they were together. 'We're going home.'

★ ★ ★

A fine rain drizzled down and the ground shone under the bright lights. Malcolm and Ellen huddled together, beneath a large, black umbrella, standing a little way from the ambulance, which waited on the tarmac.

A few feet away, a tall, thin man stood alone, hands clasped behind his back, an intent look on his face as he watched the sky.

When the plane they had all been waiting for came in to land, they moved forward. A nurse hurried ahead with a wheelchair, returning a few moments later with Dan Kirby.

The tall man stepped forward and placed his hand gently but firmly on Dan's shoulder.

'Well done, Kirby,' he said. 'Good to see you looking so well. Concentrate on getting yourself fit again, then we'll expect a full report.'

'Thank you, sir,' Dan said. 'It was good of you to come.'

'Not at all, son.' The man coughed and moved away. 'I'll be in touch.'

'Uncle Malcolm . . . ' a child's voice suddenly yelled.

Malcolm and Ellen both turned at once as Paolina came hurtling towards them, arms outstretched.

Malcolm quickly handed the umbrella to Ellen, so he could lift the girl high in the air.

Behind Paolina came Cathy, a quiet little boy held tightly in her arms.

His little face lit up in a merry smile when he saw Malcolm and, with hesitation, he put his arms out and, for the first time since their reunion, Cathy was able to let him go.

They moved aside as the rest of the passengers disembarked.

'All right, lad?' Malcolm called to Dan as he was helped into the back of the ambulance.

Dan grinned and gave a thumbs-up sign, just before the doors closed and he was locked away out of sight.

Paolina skipped ahead, twirling round and round, holding out her hands, lifting her face to the rain.

Ellen pulled Cathy under the shelter of the umbrella, and once more Malcolm embraced Paolina still holding Stefano, who was giggling with happiness.

'How are you?' Ellen whispered, her eyes full of mischief.

'I've never felt happier,' Cathy confessed.

'And Dan?'

Cathy turned and looked into Ellen's wise eyes, understanding the unspoken question.

'It's too soon.' She shook her head,

then turned to watch the ambulance as it drove way. He was all alone — he had no loving family.

'Dan's a good friend,' she said. 'I hope I'll see him again.'

'It is possible to love again, you know.' Ellen squeezed Cathy's hand, a world of understanding in her eyes. 'There was a time when I wouldn't have believed that. I don't love John any less because I'm going to marry Malcolm.

'You're still so young. Don't be afraid to live your life.'

Cathy nodded. Perhaps she would, one day, have cause to recall those words and reflect on the wisdom contained in them.

'Come on, Mummy,' Paolina cried impatiently. 'I want to get home.'

'Home!' Stefano echoed.

Cathy and Ellen hurried to catch them — Cathy not wanting to let them out of her sight, not for a moment. For she was aware that these four dear, precious people were her whole life and nothing would ever be allowed to part them again.

She turned back once and watched the ambulance as it finally turned the corner.

This wasn't the end, far from it. This was the beginning — a new beginning for all of them.

We do hope that you have enjoyed reading this large print book.

Did you know that all of our titles are available for purchase?

We publish a wide range of high quality large print books including:
**Romances, Mysteries, Classics**
**General Fiction**
**Non Fiction and Westerns**

Special interest titles available in large print are:
**The Little Oxford Dictionary**
**Music Book, Song Book**
**Hymn Book, Service Book**

Also available from us courtesy of Oxford University Press:
**Young Readers' Dictionary**
**(large print edition)**
**Young Readers' Thesaurus**
**(large print edition)**

For further information or a free brochure, please contact us at:
**Ulverscroft Large Print Books Ltd.,**
**The Green, Bradgate Road, Anstey,**
**Leicester, LE7 7FU, England.**
**Tel:** (00 44) **0116 236 4325**
**Fax:** (00 44) **0116 234 0205**

*Other titles in the*
*Linford Romance Library:*

# THE POWER AND THE PASSION

## Joyce Johnson

After a failed business venture and a broken engagement, artist Abbie Richards takes advantage of an opportunity to do a year's English teaching in Sicily. There, she becomes involved with the large, extended Puzzi family; it's members wealthy and powerfully placed in the community. Abbie enjoys the teaching and the social life at Maria Puzzi's language school, and falls in love with charismatic surgeon Roberto Puzzi, only to find herself dangerously entangled in the Puzzi power struggles . . .

# HOLD ME CLOSE

## Margaret Mounsdon

Resting actress Sara Armitage is thrilled to be offered a job, even if it means looking after Lyle Jackson's young daughter Jenny. Sara and Lyle have history and when Carla de Courcy, now Lyle's ex-wife and Jenny's mother, appears back on the scene, Sara is forced to face up to her past. Will Lyle break her heart for a second time or is she strong enough to withstand her love for him?